PRAISE FO
DOWN AND OUT IN THE M

"Fast, smart, fun, and flashy: Cory D
in the Magic Kingdom is all of the abo
able to make readers understand and even sympathize with Jules' far-out plight shows that he's got as firm a grip on human verities as on the twists and turns a technologically driven society might take."

—*The Seattle Times*

"The Singularity, or Spike, is deemed to be that moment at which mankind emerges into transhuman existence, with or without the help or hindrance of strong AI. (Doctorow eschews the AI, for the most part.) Envisioning such a future is one of the hardest tasks an SF writer can take on, but Doctorow proves himself equal to the challenge."

—Paul Di Filippo, *SF Weekly*

"Doctorow throws off cool ideas the way champagne generates bubbles . . . [he] definitely has the goods to be a major player in postcyberpunk science fiction. His ideas are fresh and his attitude highly engaging."

—*San Francisco Chronicle*

"An amazing job . . . I was so engrossed in it, I didn't want to leave."

—Wil Wheaton

"A lot of ideas are packed into this short novel, but Doctorow's own best idea was setting his story in Disney World, where it's hard to tell whether technology serves dreams or vice versa. . . . Doctorow has served up a nicely understated dish: meringue laced with caffeine."

—*Publishers Weekly*

"Cory Doctorow doesn't just write about the future—I think he lives there."

—Kelly Link, author of *Stranger Things Happen*

"*Down and Out in* ... ce
fiction novel that t ... ve
written if they ... ck
issues of *Theme P* ... —
but more importa ... are
cool, the gadgets a ... ky,
the final product is not. *Dow* ... *om*
is a sleek, tightly written book that, as the best science fiction should, engages the world."

—*Locus*

"In the true spirit of Walt Disney, Doctorow has ripped a part of our common culture, mixed it with a brilliant story, and burned into our culture a new set of memes that will be with us for a generation at least."

—Lawrence Lessig, author of *The Future of Ideas*

"Cory Doctorow rocks! *Down and Out in The Magic Kingdom* is about a world that is visible in its outlines today, if you know where to look, from reputation systems to peer-to-peer adhocracies. Doctorow knows where to look."

—Howard Rheingold, author of *Smart Mobs*

"A gripping, fast-paced story that hinges on thought-provoking extrapolation from today's technical realities. This is the sort of book that captures and defines the spirit of a turning point in human history when our tools remake ourselves and our world."

—Mitch Kapor, founder of Lotus, Inc.

"The ideas are an incredibly rich playground, and the author doesn't make you suffer through flat characters or clunky prose to get to them. On the contrary, these are totally alive characters set in a deeply conjured world . . . Highly recommended."

—Jeff Bezos, founder of Amazon.com

"Wow! Disney imagineering meets nanotechnology, the reputation economy, and Ray Kurzweil's transhuman future. As much fun as Neal Stephenson's *Snow Crash*, and as packed with mind-bending ideas about social changes cascading from the frontiers of science."

—Tim O'Reilly, publisher of O'Reilly and Associates

"Black comedic, sci-fi prophecy on the dangers of surrendering our consensual hallucination to the regime. Fun to read, but difficult to sleep afterwards."

—Douglas Rushkoff, author of *Cyberia* and *Media Virus!*

"Doctorow has created a rich and exciting vision of the future, and then wrote a page-turner of a story in it. I couldn't put the book down."

—Bruce Schneier, author of *Secrets and Lies*

Other Books by Cory Doctorow

A Place So Foreign and Eight More

The Complete Idiot's Guide to Publishing Science Fiction
(with Karl Schroeder)

Essential Blogging
(with Rael Dornfest, J. Scott Johnson, Shelly Powers,
Benjamin Trott, and Mena G. Trott)

Eastern Standard Tribe
(forthcoming)

Down and Out in the Magic Kingdom

CORY DOCTOROW

TOR®
A Tom Doherty Associates Book
New York

DOWN AND OUT IN THE MAGIC KINGDOM

Book design by Michael Collica

Edited by Patrick Nielsen Hayden

A Tor Book
Published by Tom Doherty Associates, LLC
175 Fifth Avenue
New York, NY 10010

www.tor.com

Tor® is a registered trademark of Tom Doherty Associates, LLC.

Library of Congress Cataloging-in-Publication Data

Doctorow, Cory.
Down and out in the Magic Kingdom / Cory Doctorow.
p. cm.
"A Tom Doherty Associates Book."

ISBN: 978-0-7653-0953-2

1. Walt Disney World (Fla.)—Fiction. 2. Immortalism—Fiction.
3. Florida—Fiction. I. Title.

PS3604.O38 D68 2003
813'.6—dc21
2002073277

Printed in the United States of America

D 20 19 18

I lived long enough to see the cure for death; to see the rise of the Bitchun Society; to learn ten languages; to compose three symphonies; to realize my boyhood dream of taking up residence in Disney World; to see the death of the workplace and of work.

I never thought I'd live to see the day when Keep A-Movin' Dan would decide to deadhead until the heat death of the Universe.

Dan was in his second or third blush of youth when I first met him, sometime late-XXI. He was a rangy cowpoke, apparent twenty-five or so, all rawhide squint-lines and sunburned neck, boots worn thin and infinitely comfortable. I was in the middle of my Chem thesis, my fourth Doctorate, and he was taking a break from Saving the World, chilling on campus in Toronto and core-dumping for some poor Anthro major. We hooked up at the Grad Students' Union—the GSU, or Gazoo for those who knew—on a busy Friday night, springish. I was fighting a coral-slow battle for a stool at the scratched bar, inching my way closer every time the press of bodies shifted, and he had one of the few seats, surrounded by a litter of cigarette junk and empties, clearly encamped.

Some duration into my foray, he cocked his head at me and raised a sun-bleached eyebrow. "You get any closer, son, and we're going to have to get a pre-nup."

I was apparent forty or so, and I thought about bridling at being called son, but I looked into his eyes and decided that he had enough realtime that he could call me son anytime he wanted. I backed off a little and apologized.

He struck a cig and blew a pungent, strong plume over the bartender's head. "Don't worry about it. I'm probably a little overaccustomed to personal space."

I couldn't remember the last time I'd heard anyone on-world talk about personal space. With the mortality rate at zero and the birthrate at nonzero, the world was inexorably accreting a dense carpet of people, even with the migratory and deadhead drains on the population. "You've been jaunting?" I asked—his eyes were too sharp for him to have missed an instant's experience to deadheading.

He chuckled. "No sir, not me. I'm into the kind of macho shitheadery that you only come across on-world. Jaunting's for play; I need work." The bar glass tinkled a counterpoint.

I took a moment to conjure a HUD with his Whuffie score on it. I had to resize the window—he had too many zeroes to fit on my standard display. I tried to act cool, but he caught the upwards flick of my eyes and then their involuntary widening. He tried a little aw-shucksery, gave it up and let a prideful grin show.

"I try not to pay it much mind. Some people, they get overly grateful." He must've seen my eyes flick up again, to pull his Whuffie history. "Wait, don't go doing that—I'll tell you about it, you really got to know.

"Damn, you know, it's so easy to get used to life without hyperlinks. You'd think you'd really miss 'em, but you don't."

And it clicked for me. He was a missionary—one of those fringe-dwellers who act as emissary from the Bitchun Society to the benighted corners of the world where, for whatever reasons, they want to die, starve, and choke on petrochem waste. It's amazing that these communities survive more than a generation; in the Bitchun Society proper, we usually outlive our detractors. The missionaries don't have such a high success rate—you have to be awfully convincing to get through to a culture that's already successfully resisted nearly a century's worth of propaganda—but when you convert a whole village, you accrue all the Whuffie they have to give. More often, missionaries end up getting refreshed from a backup after they aren't heard from for a decade or so. I'd never met one in the flesh before.

"How many successful missions have you had?" I asked.

"Figured it out, huh? I've just come off my fifth in twenty years—counterrevolutionaries hidden out in the old Cheyenne Mountain NORAD site, still there a generation later." He sandpapered his whiskers with his fingertips. "Their parents went to ground after their life's savings vanished, and they had no use for tech any more advanced than a rifle. Plenty of those, though."

He spun a fascinating yarn then, how he slowly gained the acceptance of the mountain-dwellers, and then their trust, and then betrayed it in subtle, beneficent ways: introducing Free Energy to their greenhouses, then a gengineered crop or two, then curing a couple deaths, slowly inching them toward the Bitchun Society, until they couldn't remember why they hadn't wanted to be a part of it from the start. Now they were mostly off-world, exploring toy frontiers with unlimited energy and unlimited supplies and deadheading through the dull times en route.

"I guess it'd be too much of a shock for them to stay on-world. They think of us as the enemy, you know—they had all kinds of plans drawn up for when we invaded them and took them away; hollow suicide teeth, booby-traps, fall-back-and-rendezvous points for the survivors. They just can't get over hating us, even though we don't even know they exist. Off-world, they can pretend that they're still living rough and hard." He rubbed his chin again, his hard calluses grating over his whiskers. "But for me, the real rough life is right here, on-world. The little enclaves, each one is like an alternate history of humanity—what if we'd taken the Free Energy, but not deadheading? What if we'd taken deadheading, but only for the critically ill, not for people who didn't want to be bored on long bus rides? Or no hyperlinks, no ad-hocracy, no Whuffie? Each one is different and wonderful."

I have a stupid habit of arguing for the sake of, and I found myself saying, "Wonderful? Oh sure, nothing finer than, oh, let's see, dying, starving, freezing, broiling, killing, cruelty and ignorance and pain and misery. I know I sure miss it."

Keep A-Movin' Dan snorted. "You think a junkie misses sobriety?"

I knocked on the bar. "Hello! There aren't any junkies anymore!"

He struck another cig. "But you know what a junkie *is*, right? Junkies don't miss sobriety, because they don't remember how sharp everything was, how the pain made the joy sweeter. We can't remember what it was like to work to earn our keep; to worry that there might not be *enough*, that we might get sick or get hit by a bus. We don't remember what it was like to take chances, and we sure as shit don't remember what it felt like to have them pay off."

He had a point. Here I was, only in my second or third adulthood, and already ready to toss it all in and do something, *anything* else. He had a point—but I wasn't about to admit it. "So you say. I say, I take a chance when I strike up a conversation in a bar, when I fall in love. . . . And what about the deadheads? Two people I know, they just went deadhead for ten thousand years! Tell me that's not taking a chance!" Truth be told, almost everyone I'd known in my eighty-some years were deadheading or jaunting or just *gone*. Lonely days, then.

"Brother, that's committing half-assed suicide. The way we're going, they'll be lucky if someone doesn't just switch 'em off when it comes time to reanimate. In case you haven't noticed, it's getting a little crowded around here."

I made pish-tosh sounds and wiped off my forehead with a bar napkin—the Gazoo was beastly hot on summer nights. "Uh-huh, just like the world was getting a little crowded a hundred years ago, before Free Energy. Like it was getting too greenhousey, too nukey, too hot or too cold. We fixed it then, we'll fix it again when the time comes. I'm gonna be here in ten thousand years, you damn betcha, but I think I'll do it the long way around."

He cocked his head again, and gave it some thought. If it had been any of the other grad students, I'd have assumed he was grepping for some bolstering factoids to support his next sally. But with him, I just knew he was thinking about it, the old-fashioned way.

"I think that if I'm still here in ten thousand years, I'm going to be crazy as hell. Ten thousand years, pal! Ten thousand years ago, the state-of-the-art was a goat. You really think you're going to be anything recognizably human in a hundred centuries? Me, I'm not interested in being a post-person. I'm going to wake up one day, and I'm going to say, 'Well, I guess I've seen about enough,' and that'll be my last day." I had seen where he was going with this, and I had stopped paying attention while I readied my response. I probably should have paid more attention. "But why? Why not just deadhead for a few centuries, see if there's anything that takes your fancy, and if not, back to sleep for a few more? Why do anything so *final*?"

He embarrassed me by making a show of thinking it over again, making me feel like I was just a half-pissed glib poltroon. "I suppose it's because nothing else is. I've always known that someday, I was going to stop moving, stop seeking, stop kicking, and have done with it. There'll come a day when I don't have anything left to do, except stop."

On campus, they called him Keep-A-Movin' Dan, because of his cowboy vibe and because of his lifestyle, and he somehow grew to take over every conversation I had for the next six months. I pinged his Whuffie a few times, and noticed that it was climbing steadily upward as he accumulated more esteem from the people he met.

I'd pretty much pissed away most of my Whuffie—all the savings from the symphonies and the first three theses—drinking myself stupid at the Gazoo, hogging library terminals, pestering profs, until I'd expended all the respect anyone had ever afforded me. All except Dan, who, for some reason, stood me to regular beers and meals and movies.

I got to feeling like I was someone special—not

everyone had a chum as exotic as Keep-A-Movin' Dan, the legendary missionary who visited the only places left that were closed to the Bitchun Society. I can't say for sure why he hung around with me. He mentioned once or twice that he'd liked my symphonies, and he'd read my Ergonomics thesis on applying theme park crowd-control techniques in urban settings, and liked what I had to say there. But I think it came down to us having a good time needling each other.

I'd talk to him about the vast carpet of the future unrolling before us, of the certainty that we would encounter alien intelligences some day, of the unimaginable frontiers open to each of us. He'd tell me that deadheading was a strong indicator that one's personal reservoir of introspection and creativity was dry; and that without struggle, there is no real victory.

This was a good fight, one we could have a thousand times without resolving. I'd get him to concede that Whuffie recaptured the true essence of money: in the old days, if you were broke but respected, you wouldn't starve; contrariwise if you were rich and hated, no sum could buy you security and peace. By measuring the thing that money really represented—your personal capital with your friends and neighbors—you more accurately gauged your success.

And then he'd lead me down a subtle, carefully baited trail that led to my allowing that while, yes, we might someday encounter alien species with wild and fabulous ways, that right now, there was a slightly depressing homogeneity to the world.

On a fine spring day, I defended my thesis to two embodied humans and one prof whose body was out for an overhaul, whose consciousness was present via speakerphone from the computer where it was resting. They all liked it. I collected my sheepskin and went out hunting for Dan in the sweet, flower-stinking streets.

He'd gone. The Anthro major he'd been torturing with his war-stories said that they'd wrapped up that morning, and he'd headed to the walled city of Tijuana, to take his shot with the descendants of a platoon of U.S. Marines who'd settled there and cut themselves off from the Bitchun Society.

So I went to Disney World.

In deference to Dan, I took the flight in realtime, in the minuscule cabin reserved for those of us who stubbornly refused to be frozen and stacked like cordwood for the two-hour flight. I was the only one taking the trip in realtime, but a flight attendant dutifully served me a urine-sample-sized orange juice and a rubbery, pungent, cheese omelet. I stared out the windows at the infinite clouds while the autopilot banked around the turbulence, and wondered when I'd see Dan next.

My girlfriend was fifteen percent of my age, and I was old-fashioned enough that it bugged me. Her name was Lil, and she was second-generation Disney World, her parents being among the original ad-hocracy that took over the management of Liberty Square and Tom Sawyer Island. She was, quite literally, raised in Walt Disney World, and it showed.

It showed. She was neat and efficient in her every little thing, from her shining red hair to her careful accounting of each gear and cog in the animatronics that were in her charge. Her folks were in canopic jars in Kissimmee, deadheading for a few centuries.

On a muggy Wednesday, we dangled our feet over the edge of the Liberty Belle's riverboat pier, watching the listless Confederate flag over Fort Langhorn on Tom Sawyer Island by moonlight. The Magic Kingdom was all closed up and every last guest had been chased out the gate underneath the Main Street train station, and we were able to breathe a heavy sigh of relief, shuck parts of our costumes, and relax together while the cicadas sang.

I was more than a century old, but there was still a kind of magic in having my arm around the warm, fine shoulders of a girl by moonlight, hidden from the hustle of the cleaning teams by the turnstiles, breathing the warm, moist air. Lil plumped her head against my shoulder and gave me a butterfly kiss under my jaw.

"Her name was McGill," I sang, gently.

"But she called herself Lil," she sang, warm breath on my collarbones.

"And everyone knew her as Nancy," I sang.

I'd been startled to know that she knew the Beatles. They'd been old news in my youth, after all. But her parents had given her a thorough—if eclectic—education.

"Want to do a walk-through?" she asked. It was one of her favorite duties, exploring every inch of the rides in her care with the lights on, after the horde of tourists had gone. We both liked to see the underpinnings of the magic. Maybe that was why I kept picking at the relationship.

"I'm a little pooped. Let's sit a while longer, if you don't mind."

She heaved a dramatic sigh. "Oh, all right. Old man." She reached up and gently tweaked my nipple, and I gave a satisfying little jump. I think the age difference bothered her, too, though she teased me for letting it get to me.

"I think I'll be able to manage a totter through the Haunted Mansion, if you just give me a moment to rest my bursitis." I felt her smile against my shirt. She loved the Mansion; loved to turn on the ballroom ghosts and dance their waltz with them on the dusty floor, loved to try and stare down the marble busts in the library that followed your gaze as you passed.

I liked it too, but I really liked just sitting there with her, watching the water and the trees. I was just getting ready to go when I heard a soft *ping* inside my cochlea. "Damn," I said. "I've got a call."

"Tell them you're busy," she said.

"I will," I said, and answered the call subvocally. "Julius here."

"Hi, Julius. It's Dan. You got a minute?"

I knew a thousand Dans, but I recognized the voice immediately, though it'd been ten years since we last got drunk at the Gazoo together. I muted the subvocal and said, "Lil, I've got to take this. Do you mind?"

"Oh, *no,* not at all," she sarcased at me. She sat up and pulled out her crack pipe and lit up.

"Dan," I subvocalized, "long time no speak."

"Yeah, buddy, it sure has been," he said, and his voice cracked on a sob.

I turned and gave Lil such a look, she dropped her pipe. "How can I help?" she said, softly but swiftly. I waved her off and switched the phone to full-vocal mode. My voice sounded unnaturally loud in the cricket-punctuated calm.

"Where you at, Dan?" I asked.

"Down here, in Orlando. I'm stuck out on Pleasure Island."

"All right," I said. "Meet me at, uh, the Adventurer's Club, upstairs on the couch by the door. I'll be there in—" I shot a look at Lil, who knew the castmember-only roads better than I. She flashed ten fingers at me. "Ten minutes."

"OK," he said. "Sorry." He had his voice back under control. I switched off.

"What's up?" Lil asked.

"I'm not sure. An old friend is in town. He sounds like he's got a problem."

Lil pointed a finger at me and made a trigger-squeezing gesture. "There," she said. "I've just dumped the best route to Pleasure Island to your public directory. Keep me in the loop, okay?"

I set off for the utilidor entrance near the Hall of Presidents and booted down the stairs to the hum of the underground tunnel-system. I took the slidewalk to cast parking and zipped my little cart out to Pleasure Island.

I found Dan sitting on the L-shaped couch underneath rows of faked-up trophy shots with humorous captions. Downstairs, castmembers were working the animatronic masks and idols, chattering with the guests.

Dan was apparent fifty-plus, a little paunchy and stubbled. He had raccoon-mask bags under his eyes and he slumped listlessly. As I approached, I pinged his Whuffie and was startled to see that it had dropped to nearly zero.

"Jesus," I said, as I sat down next to him. "You look like hell, Dan."

He nodded. "Appearances can be deceptive," he said. "But in this case, they're bang-on."

"You want to talk about it?" I asked.

"Somewhere else, huh? I hear they ring in the New Year every night at midnight; I think that'd be a little too much for me right now."

I led him out to my cart and cruised back to the place I shared with Lil, out in Kissimmee. He smoked eight cigarettes on the twenty minute ride, hammering one after another into his mouth, filling my runabout with stinging clouds. I kept glancing at him in the rear-view. He had his eyes closed, and in repose he looked dead. I could hardly believe that this was my vibrant action-hero pal of yore.

Surreptitiously, I called Lil's phone. "I'm bringing him home," I subvocalized. "He's in rough shape. Not sure what it's all about."

"I'll make up the couch," she said. "And get some coffee together. Love you."

"Back atcha, kid," I said.

As we approached the tacky little swaybacked ranch house, he opened his eyes. "You're a pal, Jules." I waved him off. "No, really. I tried to think of who I could call, and you were the only one. I've missed you, bud."

"Lil said she'd put some coffee on," I said. "You sound like you need it."

Lil was waiting on the sofa, a folded blanket and an extra pillow on the side table, a pot of coffee and some Disneyland Beijing mugs beside them. She stood and extended her hand. "I'm Lil," she said.

"Dan," he said. "It's a pleasure."

I knew she was pinging his Whuffie and I caught her look of surprised disapproval. Us oldsters who predate Whuffie know that it's important; but to the kids, it's the *world.* Someone without any is automatically suspect. I watched her recover quickly, smile, and surreptitiously wipe her hand on her jeans. "Coffee?" she said.

"Oh, yeah," Dan said, and slumped on the sofa.

She poured him a cup and set it on a coaster on the coffee table. "I'll let you boys catch up, then," she said, and started for the bedroom.

"No," Dan said. "Wait. If you don't mind. I think it'd help if I could talk to someone . . . younger, too."

She set her face in the look of chirpy helpfulness that all the second-gen castmembers have at their instant disposal, and settled into an armchair. She pulled out her pipe and lit a rock. I went through my crack period before she was born, just after they made it decaf, and I always felt old when I saw her and her friends light up. Dan surprised me by holding out a hand to her and taking the pipe. He toked heavily, then passed it back.

Dan closed his eyes again, then ground his fists into

them, sipped his coffee. It was clear he was trying to figure out where to start.

"I believed that I was braver than I really am, is what it boils down to," he said.

"Who doesn't?" I said.

"I really thought I could do it. I knew that someday I'd run out of things to do, things to see. I knew that I'd finish some day. You remember, we used to argue about it. I swore I'd be done, and that would be the end of it. And now I am. There isn't a single place left on-world that isn't part of the Bitchun Society. There isn't a single thing left that I want any part of."

"So deadhead for a few centuries," I said. "Put the decision off."

"No!" he shouted, startling both of us. "I'm *done*. It's *over.*"

"So do it," Lil said.

"I *can't,*" he sobbed, and buried his face in his hands. He cried like a baby, in great, snoring sobs that shook his whole body. Lil went into the kitchen and got some tissue, and passed it to me. I sat alongside him and awkwardly patted his back.

"Jesus," he said, into his palms. "Jesus."

"Dan?" I said, quietly.

He sat up and took the tissue, wiped off his face and hands. "Thanks," he said. "I've tried to make a go of it, really I have. I've spent the last eight years in Istanbul, writing papers on my missions, about the communities. I did some followup studies, interviews. No one was interested. Not even me. I smoked a lot of hash. It didn't help. So, one morning I woke up and went to the bazaar and said good-bye to the friends I'd made there. Then I went to a pharmacy and had the man make me up a lethal injection. He wished me good luck and I went back to my rooms. I sat there with the hypo all afternoon, then I decided to sleep on it, and I got up the next morning and did it all over again. I looked inside myself, and I saw that I didn't have the guts. I just didn't have the guts. I've stared down the barrels of a hundred guns, had a thousand knives pressed up against my throat, but I didn't have the guts to press that button."

"You were too late," Lil said.

We both turned to look at her.

"You were a decade too late. Look at you. You're pathetic. If you killed yourself right now, you'd just be a washed-up loser who couldn't hack it. If you'd done it ten years earlier, you would've been going out on top—a champion, retiring permanently." She set her mug down with a harder-than-necessary clunk.

Sometimes, Lil and I are right on the same wavelength. Sometimes, it's like she's on a different planet. All I could do was sit there, horrified, and she was happy to discuss the timing of my pal's suicide.

But she was right. Dan nodded heavily, and I saw that he knew it, too.

"A day late and a dollar short," he sighed.

"Well, don't just sit there," she said. "You know what you've got to do."

"What?" I said, involuntarily irritated by her tone.

She looked at me like I was being deliberately stupid. "He's got to get back on top. Cleaned up, dried out, into some productive work. Get that Whuffie up, too. *Then* he can kill himself with dignity."

It was the stupidest thing I'd ever heard. Dan, though, was cocking an eyebrow at her and thinking hard. "How old did you say you were?" he asked.

"Twenty-three," she said.

"Wish I'd had your smarts at twenty-three," he said, and heaved a sigh, straightening up. "Can I stay here while I get the job done?"

I looked askance at Lil, who considered for a moment, then nodded.

"Sure, pal, sure," I said. I clapped him on the shoulder. "You look beat."

"Beat doesn't begin to cover it," he said.

"Good night, then," I said.

Ad-hocracy works well, for the most part. Lil's folks had taken over the running of Liberty Square with a group of other interested, compatible souls. They did a fine job, racked up gobs of Whuffie, and anyone who came around and tried to take it over would be so reviled by the guests they wouldn't find a pot to piss in. Or they'd have such a wicked, radical approach that they'd ouster Lil's parents and their pals, and do a better job.

It can break down, though. There were pretenders to the throne—a group who'd worked with the original ad-hocracy and then had moved off to other pursuits—some of them had gone to school, some of them had made movies, written books, or gone off to Disneyland Beijing to help start things up. A few had deadheaded for a couple decades.

They came back to Liberty Square with a message: update the attractions. The Liberty Square ad-hocs were the staunchest conservatives in the Magic Kingdom, preserving the wheezing technology in the face of a Park that changed almost daily. The newcomer/old-timers were on-side with the rest of the Park, had their support, and looked like they might make a successful go of it.

So it fell to Lil to make sure that there were no bugs in the meager attractions of Liberty Square: the Hall of the Presidents, the Liberty Belle riverboat, and the glorious Haunted Mansion, arguably the coolest attraction to come from the fevered minds of the old-time Disney Imagineers.

I caught her backstage at the Hall of the Presidents, tinkering with Lincoln II, the backup animatronic. Lil tried to keep two of everything running at speed, just in case. She could swap out a dead bot for a backup in five minutes flat, which is all that crowd-control would permit.

It had been two weeks since Dan's arrival, and though I'd barely seen him in that time, his presence was vivid in our lives. Our little ranch-house had a new smell, not unpleasant, of rejuve and hope and loss, something barely noticeable over the tropical flowers nodding in front of our porch. My phone rang three or four times a day, Dan checking in from his rounds of the Park, seeking out some way to accumulate personal capital. His excitement and dedication to the task were inspiring, pulling me into his over-the-top-and-damn-the-torpedoes mode of being.

"You just missed Dan," she said. She had her head in Lincoln's chest, working with an autosolder and a magnifier. Bent over, red hair tied back in a neat bun, sweat sheening her wiry freckled arms, smelling of girl-sweat and machine lubricant, she made me wish there were a mattress somewhere backstage. I settled for patting her behind affectionately, and she wriggled appreciatively. "He's looking better."

His rejuve had taken him back to apparent twenty-five, the way I remembered him. He was rawboned and leathery, but still had the defeated stoop that had startled me when I saw him at the Adventurer's Club. "What did he want?"

"He's been hanging out with Debra—he wanted to make sure I knew what she's up to."

Debra was one of the old guard, a former comrade of Lil's parents. She'd spent a decade in Disneyland Beijing, coding sim-rides. If she had her way, we'd tear down every marvelous Rube Goldberg in the Park and replace them with pristine white sim boxes on giant, articulated servos.

The problem was that she was *really good* at coding sims. Her Great Movie Ride rehab at MGM was breathtaking—the Star Wars sequence had already inspired a hundred fan-sites that fielded millions of hits.

She'd leveraged her success into a deal with the Adventureland ad-hocs to rehab the Pirates of the Caribbean, and their backstage areas were piled high with reference: treasure chests and cutlasses and bowsprits. It was terrifying to walk through; the Pirates was the last ride Walt personally supervised, and we'd thought it was sacrosanct. But Debra had built a Pirates sim in Beijing, based on Chend I Sao, the XIXth century Chinese pirate queen, which was credited with rescuing the Park from obscurity and ruin. The Florida iteration would incorporate the best aspects of its Chinese cousin—the AI-driven sims that communicated with each other and with the guests, greeting them by name each time they rode and spinning age-appropriate tales of piracy on the high seas; the spectacular fly-through of the aquatic necropolis of rotting junks on the sea-floor; the thrilling pitch and yaw of the sim as it weathered a violent, breathtaking storm—but with Western themes: wafts of Jamaican pepper sauce crackling through the air; liquid Afro-Caribbean accents; and swordfights conducted in the manner of the pirates who plied the blue waters of the New World. Identical sims would stack like cordwood in the space currently occupied by the bulky ride-apparatus and dioramas, quintupling capacity and halving load-time.

"So, what's she up to?"

Lil extracted herself from the Rail-Splitter's mechanical guts and made a comical moue of worry. "She's rehabbing the Pirates—and doing an incredible job. They're ahead of schedule, they've got good net-buzz, the focus groups are cumming themselves." The comedy went out of her expression, baring genuine worry.

She turned away and closed up Honest Abe, then fired her finger at him. Smoothly, he began to run through his spiel, silent but for the soft hum and whine of his servos. Lil mimed twiddling a knob and his audiotrack kicked in low: "All the armies of Europe, Asia, and Africa *combined* could not, by force, make a track on the Blue Ridge, nor take a drink from the Ohio. If destruction be our lot, then we ourselves must be its author—and its finisher." She mimed turning down the gain and he fell silent again.

"You said it, Mr. President," she said, and fired her finger at him again, powering him down. She bent and adjusted his hand-sewn period topcoat, then carefully wound and set the turnip-watch in his vest-pocket.

I put my arm around her shoulders. "You're doing all you can—and it's good work," I said. I'd fallen into the easy castmember mode of speaking, voicing bland affirmations. Hearing the words, I felt a flush of embarrassment. I pulled her into a long, hard hug and fumbled for better reassurance. Finding no words that would do, I gave her a final squeeze and let her go.

She looked at me sidelong and nodded her head. "It'll be fine, of course," she said. "I mean, the worst possible scenario is that Debra will do her job very, very well, and make things even better than they are now. That's not so bad."

This was a 180-degree reversal of her position on the subject the last time we'd talked, but you don't live more than a century without learning when to point out that sort of thing and when not to.

My cochlea struck twelve noon and a HUD appeared with my weekly backup reminder. Lil was maneuvering Ben Franklin II out of his niche. I waved good-bye at her back and walked away, to an uplink terminal. Once I was close enough for secure broadband communications, I got ready to back up. My cochlea chimed again and I answered it.

"Yes," I subvocalized, impatiently. I hated getting distracted from a backup—one of my enduring fears was that I'd forget the backup altogether and leave myself vulnerable for an entire week until the next reminder. I'd lost the knack of getting into habits in my adolescence, giving in completely to machine-generated reminders over conscious choice.

"It's Dan." I heard the sound of the Park in full swing behind him—children's laughter; bright, recorded animatronic spiels; the tromp of thousands of feet. "Can you meet me at the Tiki Room? It's pretty important."

"Can it wait for fifteen?" I asked.

"Sure—see you in fifteen."

I rung off and initiated the backup. A status-bar zipped across a HUD, dumping the parts of my memory that were purely digital; then it finished and started in on organic memory. My eyes rolled back in my head and my life flashed before my eyes.

The Bitchun Society has had much experience with restores from backup—in the era of the cure for death, people live pretty recklessly. Some people get refreshed a couple dozen times a year.

Not me. I hate the process. Not so much that I won't participate in it. Everyone who had serious philosophical conundra on that subject just, you know, *died,* a generation before. The Bitchun Society didn't need to convert its detractors, just outlive them.

The first time I died, it was not long after my sixtieth birthday. I was SCUBA diving at Playa Coral, near Veradero, Cuba. Of course, I don't remember the incident, but knowing my habits at that particular dive-site and having read the dive-logs of my SCUBA-buddies, I've reconstructed the events.

I was eeling my way through the lobster-caves, with a borrowed bottle and mask. I'd also borrowed a wetsuit, but I wasn't wearing it—the blood-temp salt water was balm, and I hated erecting barriers between it and my skin. The caves were made of coral and rocks, and they coiled and twisted like intestines. Through each hole and around each corner, there was a hollow, rough sphere of surpassing alien beauty. Giant lobsters skittered over the walls and through the holes. Schools of fish as bright as jewels darted and executed breathtaking precision maneuvers as I disturbed their busy days. I do some of my best thinking under water, and I'm often slipping off into dangerous reverie at depth. Normally, my diving buddies ensure that I don't hurt myself, but this time I got away from them, spidering forward into a tiny hole.

Where I got stuck.

My diving buddies were behind me, and I rapped on my bottle with the hilt of my knife until one of them put a hand on my shoulder. My buddies saw what was up, and attempted to pull me loose, but my bottle and buoyancy-control vest were firmly wedged. The others exchanged hand signals, silently debating the best way to get me loose. Suddenly, I was thrashing and kicking, and then I disappeared into the cave, minus my vest and bottle. I'd apparently attempted to cut through my vest's straps and managed to sever the tube of my regulator. After inhaling a jolt of sea water, I'd thrashed free into the cave, rolling into a monstrous patch of spindly fire-coral. I'd inhaled another lungful of water and kicked madly for a tiny hole in the cave's ceiling, whence my buddies retrieved me shortly thereafter, drowned-blue except for the patchy red welts from the stinging coral.

In those days, making a backup was a lot more complicated; the procedure took most of a day, and had to be undertaken at a special clinic. Luckily, I'd had one made just before I left for Cuba, a few weeks earlier. My next-most-recent backup was three years old, dating from the completion of my second symphony.

They recovered me from backup and into a force-grown clone at Toronto General. As far as I knew, I'd laid down in the backup clinic one moment and arisen the next. It took most of a year to get over the feeling that the whole world was putting a monstrous joke over on me, that the drowned corpse I'd seen was indeed my own. In my mind, the rebirth was figurative as well as literal—the missing time was enough that I found myself hard-pressed to socialize with my pre-death friends.

I told Dan the story during our first friendship, and he immediately pounced on the fact that I'd gone to Disney World to spend a week sorting out my feelings, reinventing myself, moving to space, marrying a crazy lady. He found it very curious that I always rebooted myself at Disney World. When I told him that I was going to live there someday, he asked me if that would mean that I was done reinventing myself. Sometimes, as I ran my fingers through Lil's sweet red curls, I thought of that remark and sighed great gusts of contentment and marveled that my friend Dan had been so prescient.

The next time I died, they'd improved the technology somewhat. I'd had a massive stroke in my seventy-third year, collapsing on the ice in the middle of a house-league hockey game. By the time they cut my helmet away, the hematomae had crushed my brain into a pulpy, blood-sotted mess. I'd been lax in backing up, and I lost most of a year. But they woke me gently, with a computer-generated precis of the events of the missing interval, and a counselor contacted me daily for a year until I felt at home again in my skin. Again, my life rebooted, and I found myself in Disney World, methodically flensing away the relationships I'd built and starting afresh in Boston, living on the ocean floor and working the heavy-metal harvesters, a project that led, eventually, to my Chem thesis at U of T.

After I was shot dead at the Tiki Room, I had the opportunity to appreciate the great leaps that restores had made in the intervening ten years. I woke in my own bed, instantly aware of the events that led up to my third death as seen from various third-party POVs: security footage from the Adventureland cameras, synthesized memories extracted from Dan's own backup, and a computer-generated fly-through of the scene. I woke feeling preternaturally calm and cheerful, and knowing that I felt that way because of certain temporary neurotransmitter presets that had been put in place when I was restored.

Dan and Lil sat at my bedside. Lil's tired, smiling face was limned with hairs that had snuck loose of her ponytail. She took my hand and kissed the smooth knuckles. Dan smiled beneficently at me and I was seized with a warm, comforting feeling of being surrounded by people who really loved me. I dug for words appropriate to the scene, decided to wing it, opened my mouth and said, to my surprise, "I have to pee."

Dan and Lil smiled at each other. I lurched out of the bed, naked, and thumped to the bathroom. My muscles were wonderfully limber, with a brand new spring to them. After I flushed I leaned over and took hold of my ankles, then pulled my head right to the floor, feeling the marvelous flexibility of my back and legs and buttocks. A scar on my knee was missing, as were the many lines that had crisscrossed my fingers. When I looked in the mirror, I saw that my nose and earlobes were smaller and perkier. The familiar crow's-feet and the frown lines between my eyebrows were gone. I had a day's beard all over—head, face, pubis, arms, legs. I ran my hands over my body and chuckled at the ticklish newness of it all. I was briefly tempted to depilate all over, just to keep this feeling of newness forever, but the neurotransmitter presets were evaporating and a sense of urgency over my murder was creeping up on me.

I tied a towel around my waist and made my way back to the bedroom. The smells of tile cleaner and flowers and rejuve were bright in my nose, effervescent as camphor. Dan and Lil stood when I came into the room and helped me to the bed. "Well, this *sucks,*" I said.

I'd gone straight from the uplink through the utilidors—three quick cuts of security cam footage, one at the uplink, one in the corridor, and one at the exit in the underpass between Liberty Square and Adventureland. I seemed bemused and a little sad as I emerged from the door and began to weave my way through the crowd, using a kind of sinuous, darting shuffle that I'd developed when I was doing fieldwork on my crowd-control thesis. I cut rapidly through the lunchtime crowd toward the long roof of the Tiki Room, thatched with strips of shimmering aluminum cut and painted to look like long grass.

Fuzzy shots now, from Dan's POV, of me moving closer to him, passing close to a group of teenaged girls with extra elbows and knees, wearing environmentally controlled cloaks and cowls covered with Epcot Center logomarks. One of them is wearing a pith helmet, from the Jungle Traders shop outside of the Jungle Cruise. Dan's gaze flicks away, to the Tiki Room's entrance, where there is a short queue of older men, then back, just as the girl with the pith helmet draws a stylish little organic pistol, like a penis with a tail that coils around her arm. Casually, grinning, she raises her arm and gestures with the pistol, exactly like Lil does with her finger when she's uploading, and the pistol lunges forward. Dan's gaze flicks back to me. I'm pitching over, my lungs bursting out of my chest and spreading before me like wings, spinal gristle and viscera showering the guests before me. A piece of my nametag, now shrapnel, strikes Dan in the forehead, causing him to blink. When he looks again, the group of girls is still there, but the girl with the pistol is long gone.

The fly-through is far less confused. Everyone except me, Dan and the girl is grayed-out. We're limned in highlighter yellow, moving in slow motion. I emerge from the underpass and the girl moves from the Swiss Family Robinson Treehouse to the group of her friends; Dan starts to move towards me. The girl raises arms and fires her pistol. The self-guiding smart-slug, keyed to my body chemistry, flies low, near ground level, weaving between the feet of the crowd, moving just below the speed of sound. When it reaches me, it screams upwards and into my spine, detonating once it's entered my chest cavity.

The girl has already made a lot of ground, back toward the Adventureland/Main Street, USA gateway. The fly-through speeds up, following her as she merges with the crowds on the street, ducking and weaving between them, moving toward the breezeway at Sleeping Beauty Castle. She vanishes, then reappears, forty minutes later, in Tomorrowland, near the new Space Mountain complex, then disappears again.

"Has anyone ID'd the girl?" I asked, once I'd finished reliving the events. The anger was starting to boil within me now. My new fists clenched for the first time, soft palms and uncallused fingertips.

Dan shook his head. "None of the girls she was with had ever seen her before. The face was one of the Seven Sisters—Hope." The Seven Sisters were a trendy collection of designer faces. Every second teenage girl wore one of them.

"How about Jungle Traders?" I asked. "Did they have a record of the pith helmet purchase?"

Lil frowned. "We ran the Jungle Traders purchases back for six months: only three matched the girl's apparent age; all three have alibis. Chances are she stole it."

"Why?" I asked, finally. In my mind's eye, I saw my lungs bursting out of my chest, like wings, like jellyfish, vertebrae spraying like shrapnel. I saw the girl's smile, an almost sexual smirk as she pulled the trigger on me.

"It wasn't random," Lil said. "The slug was definitely keyed to you—that means that she'd gotten close to you at some point."

Right—which meant that she'd been to Disney World in the last ten years. That narrowed it down, all right.

"What happened to her after Tomorrowland?" I said.

"We don't know," Lil said. "Something wrong with the cameras. We lost her and she never reappeared." She sounded hot and angry—she took equipment failures in the Magic Kingdom personally.

"Who'd want to do this?" I asked, hating the self-pity in my voice. It was the first time I'd been murdered, but I didn't need to be a drama queen about it.

Dan's eyes got a faraway look. "Sometimes, people do things for reasons that seem perfectly reasonable to them, that the rest of the world couldn't hope to understand. I've seen a few assassinations, and they never made sense afterwards." He stroked his chin. "Sometimes, it's better to look for temperament, rather than motivation: who *could* do something like this?"

Right. All we needed to do was investigate all the psychopaths who'd visited the Magic Kingdom in ten years. That narrowed it down considerably. I pulled up a HUD and checked the time. It had been four days since my murder. I had a shift coming up, working the turnstiles at the Haunted Mansion. I liked to pull a couple of those shifts a month, just to keep myself grounded; it helped to take a reality check while I was churning away in the rarified climate of my crowd-control simulations.

I stood and went to my closet, started to dress.

"*What* are you doing?" Lil asked, alarmed.

"I've got a shift. I'm running late."

"You're in no shape to work," Lil said, tugging at my elbow. I jerked free of her.

"I'm fine—good as new." I barked a humorless laugh. "I'm not going to let those bastards disrupt my life any more."

Those bastards? I thought—when had I decided that there was more than one? But I knew it was true. There was no way that this was all planned by one person: it had been executed too precisely, too thoroughly.

Dan moved to block the bedroom door. "Wait a second," he said. "You need rest."

I fixed him with a doleful glare. "I'll decide that," I said. He stepped aside.

"I'll tag along, then," he said. "Just in case."

I pinged my Whuffie. I was up a couple percentiles—sympathy Whuffie—but it was falling: Dan and Lil were radiating disapproval. Screw 'em.

I got into my runabout and Dan scrambled for the passenger door as I put it in gear and sped out.

"Are you sure you're all right?" Dan said as I nearly rolled the runabout taking the corner at the end of our cul-de-sac.

"Why wouldn't I be?" I said. "I'm as good as new."

"Funny choice of words," he said. "Some would say that you *were* new."

I groaned. "Not this argument again," I said. "I feel like me and no one else is making that claim. Who cares if I've been restored from a backup?"

"All I'm saying is, there's a difference between *you* and an exact copy of you, isn't there?"

I knew what he was doing, distracting me with one of our old fights, but I couldn't resist the bait, and as I marshaled my arguments, it actually helped calm me down some. Dan was that kind of friend, a person who knew you better than you knew yourself. "So you're saying that if you were obliterated and then recreated, atom-for-atom, that you wouldn't be you anymore?"

"For the sake of argument, sure. Being destroyed

and recreated is different from not being destroyed at all, right?"

"Brush up on your quantum mechanics, pal. You're being destroyed and recreated a trillion times a second."

"On a very, very small level—"

"What difference does that make?"

"Fine, I'll concede that. But you're not really an atom-for-atom copy. You're a clone, with a copied *brain*—that's not the same as quantum destruction."

"Very nice thing to say to someone who's just been murdered, pal. You got a problem with clones?"

And we were off and running.

The Mansion's cast were sickeningly cheerful and solicitous. Each of them made a point of coming around and touching the stiff, starched shoulder of my butler's costume, letting me know that if there was anything they could do for me . . . I gave them all a fixed smile and tried to concentrate on the guests, how they waited, when they arrived, how they dispersed through the exit gate. Dan hovered nearby, occasionally taking the eight minute, twenty-two second ride-through, running interference for me with the other castmembers.

He was nearby when my break came up. I changed into civvies and we walked over the cobbled streets, past the Hall of the Presidents, noting as I rounded the corner that there was something different about the queue-area. Dan groaned. "They did it already," he said.

I looked closer. The turnstiles were blocked by a sandwich board: Mickey in a Ben Franklin wig and bifocals, holding a trowel. "Excuse our mess!" the sign declared. "We're renovating to serve you better!"

I spotted one of Debra's cronies standing behind the sign, a self-satisfied smile on his face. He'd started off life as a squat, northern Chinese, but had had his bones lengthened and his cheekbones raised so that he looked almost elfin. I took one look at his smile and understood—Debra had established a toehold in Liberty Square.

"They filed plans for the new Hall with the steering committee an hour after you got shot. The committee loved the plans; so did the net. They're promising not to touch the Mansion."

"You didn't mention this," I said, hotly.

"We thought you'd jump to conclusions. The timing was bad, but there's no indication that they arranged for the shooter. Everyone's got an alibi; furthermore, they've all offered to submit their backups for proof."

"Right," I said. "Right. So they just *happened* to have plans for a new Hall standing by. And they just *happened* to file them after I got shot, when all our ad-hocs were busy worrying about me. It's all a big coincidence."

Dan shook his head. "We're not stupid, Jules. No one thinks that it's a coincidence. Debra's the sort of person who keeps a lot of plans standing by, just in case. But that just makes her a well-prepared opportunist, not a murderer."

I felt nauseated and exhausted. I was enough of a castmember that I sought out a utilidor before I collapsed against a wall, head down. Defeat seeped through me, saturating me.

Dan crouched down beside me. I looked over at him. He was grinning wryly. "Posit," he said, "for the moment, that Debra really did do this thing, set you up so that she could take over."

I smiled, in spite of myself. This was his explaining act, the thing he would do whenever I fell into one of his rhetorical tricks back in the old days. "All right, I've posited it."

"Why would she: one, take out you instead of Lil or one of the real old-timers; two, go after the Hall of Presidents instead of Tom Sawyer Island or even the Mansion; and three, follow it up with such a blatant, suspicious move?"

"All right," I said, warming to the challenge. "One: I'm important enough to be disruptive but not so important as to rate a full investigation. Two: Tom Sawyer Island is too visible, you can't rehab it without people seeing the dust from shore. Three: Debra's coming off of a decade in Beijing, where subtlety isn't real important."

"Sure," Dan said, "sure." Then he launched an answering salvo, and while I was thinking up my answer, he helped me to my feet and walked me out to my runabout, arguing all the way, so that by the time I noticed we weren't at the Park anymore, I was home and in bed.

With all the Hall's animatronics mothballed for the duration, Lil had more time on her hands than she knew what to do with. She hung around the little bungalow, the two of us in the living room, staring blankly at the windows, breathing shallowly in the claustrophobic, superheated Florida air. I had my working notes on queue management for the Mansion, and I pecked at them aimlessly. Sometimes, Lil mirrored my HUD so she could watch me work, and made suggestions based on her long experience.

It was a delicate process, this business of increasing throughput without harming the guest experience. But for every second I could shave off of the queue-to-exit time, I could put another sixty guests through and lop thirty seconds off total wait-time. And the more guests who got to experience the Mansion, the more of a Whuffie-hit Debra's people would suffer if they made a move on it. So I dutifully pecked at my notes, and found three seconds I could shave off the graveyard sequence by swiveling the Doom Buggy carriages stage-left as they descended from the attic window: by expanding their fields-of-vision, I could expose the guests to all the scenes more quickly.

I ran the change in fly-through, then implemented it after closing, and invited the other Liberty Square ad-hocs to come and test it out.

It was another muggy winter evening, prematurely dark. The ad-hocs had enough friends and family with them that we were able to simulate an off-peak queue-time, and we all stood and sweated in the preshow area, waiting for the doors to swing open, listening to the wolf cries and assorted boo-spookery from the hidden speakers.

The doors swung open, revealing Lil in a rotting maid's uniform, her eyes lined with black, her skin powdered to a deathly pallor. She gave us a cold, considering glare, then intoned, "Master Gracey requests more bodies."

As we crowded into the cool, musty gloom of the parlor, Lil contrived to give my ass an affectionate squeeze. I turned to return the favor, and saw Debra's elfin comrade looming over Lil's shoulder. My smile died on my lips.

The man locked eyes with me for a moment, and I saw something in there—some admixture of cruelty and worry that I didn't know what to make of. He looked away immediately. I'd known that Debra would have spies in the crowd, of course, but with elf-boy watching, I resolved to make this the best show I knew how.

It's subtle, this business of making the show better from within. Lil had already slid aside the paneled wall that led to stretch-room number two, the most recently serviced one. Once the crowd had moved inside, I tried to lead their eyes by adjusting my body language to poses of subtle attention directed at the new spotlights. When the newly remastered soundtrack came from behind the sconce-bearing gargoyles at the corners of the octagonal room, I leaned my body slightly in the direction of the moving stereo-image. And an instant before the lights snapped out, I ostentatiously cast my eyes up into the scrim ceiling, noting that others had taken my cue, so they were watching when the UV-lit corpse dropped from the pitch-dark ceiling, jerking against the noose at its neck.

The crowd filed into the second queue area, where they boarded the Doom Buggies. There was a low buzz of marveling conversation as we made our way onto the moving sidewalk. I boarded my Doom Buggy and an instant later, someone slid in beside me. It was the elf.

He made a point of not making eye contact with me, but I sensed his sidelong glances at me as we rode through past the floating chandelier and into the corridor where the portraits' eyes watched us. Two years before, I'd accelerated this sequence and added some random swivel to the Doom Buggies, shaving twenty-five seconds off the total, taking the hourly throughput cap from 2365 to 2600. It was the proof-of-concept that led to all the other seconds I'd shaved away since. The violent pitching of the Buggy brought me and the elf into inadvertent contact with one another, and when I brushed his hand as I reached for the safety bar, I felt that it was cold and sweaty.

He was nervous! *He* was nervous. What did *he* have

to be nervous about? I was the one who'd been murdered—maybe he was nervous because he was supposed to finish the job. I cast my own sidelong looks at him, trying to see suspicious bulges in his tight clothes, but the Doom Buggy's pebbled black plastic interior was too dim. Dan was in the Buggy behind us, with one of the Mansion's regular castmembers. I rang his cochlea and subvocalized: "Get ready to jump out on my signal." Anyone leaving a Buggy would interrupt an infrared beam and stop the ride system. I knew I could rely on Dan to trust me without a lot of explaining, which meant that I could keep a close watch on Debra's crony.

We went past the hallway of mirrors and into the hallway of doors, where monstrous hands peeked out around the sills, straining against the hinges, recorded groans mixed in with pounding. I thought about it—if I wanted to kill someone on the Mansion, what would be the best place to do it? The attic staircase—the next sequence—seemed like a good bet. A cold clarity washed over me. The elf would kill me in the gloom of the staircase, dump me out over the edge at the blind turn toward the graveyard, and that would be it. Would he be able to do it if I were staring straight at him? He seemed terribly nervous as it was. I swiveled in my seat and looked him straight in the eye.

He quirked half a smile at me and nodded a greeting. I kept on staring at him, my hands balled into fists, ready for anything. We rode down the staircase, facing up, listening to the clamour of voices from the cemetery and the squawk of the red-eyed raven. I caught sight of the quaking groundkeeper animatronic from the corner of my eye and startled. I let out a subvocal squeal and was pitched forward as the ride system shuddered to a stop.

"Jules?" came Dan's voice in my cochlea. "You all right?"

He'd heard my involuntary note of surprise and had leapt clear of the Buggy, stopping the ride. The elf was looking at me with a mixture of surprise and pity.

"It's all right, it's all right. False alarm." I paged Lil and subvocalized to her, telling her to start up the ride ASAP, it was all right.

I rode the rest of the way with my hands on the safety bar, my eyes fixed ahead of me, steadfastly ignoring the elf. I checked the timer I'd been running. The demo was a debacle—instead of shaving off three seconds, I'd added thirty. I wanted to cry.

I debarked the Buggy and stalked quickly out of the exit queue, leaning heavily against the fence, staring blindly at the pet cemetery. My head swam: I was out of control, jumping at shadows. I was spooked.

And I had no reason to be. Sure, I'd been murdered, but what had it cost me? A few days of "unconsciousness" while they decanted my backup into my new body, a merciful gap in memory from my departure at the backup terminal up until my death. I wasn't one of those nuts who took death *seriously.* It wasn't like they'd done something *permanent.*

In the meantime, I *had* done something permanent: I'd dug Lil's grave a little deeper, endangered the adhocracy and, worst of all, the Mansion. I'd acted like an idiot. I tasted my dinner, a wolfed-down hamburger, and swallowed hard, forcing down the knob of nausea.

I sensed someone at my elbow, and thinking it was Lil, come to ask me what had gone on, I turned with a sheepish grin and found myself facing the elf.

He stuck his hand out and spoke in the flat no-accent of someone running a language module. "Hi there. We haven't been introduced, but I wanted to tell you how much I enjoy your work. I'm Tim Fung."

I pumped his hand, which was still cold and particularly clammy in the close heat of the Florida night. "Julius," I said, startled at how much like a bark it sounded. *Careful,* I thought, *no need to escalate the hostilities.* "It's kind of you to say that. I like what you-all have done with the Pirates."

He smiled: a genuine, embarrassed smile, as though he'd just been given high praise from one of his heroes. "Really? I think it's pretty good—the second time around you get a lot of chances to refine things, really clarify the vision. Beijing—well, it was exciting, but it was rushed, you know? I mean, we were really struggling. Every day, there was another pack of squatters who wanted to tear the Park down. Debra used to send me out to give the children piggyback rides, just to keep our Whuffie up while she was evicting the squatters. It was good to have the opportunity to refine the designs, revisit them without the floor show."

I knew about this, of course—Beijing had been a real struggle for the ad-hocs who built it. Lots of them had been killed, many times over. Debra herself had been killed every day for a week and restored to a series of prepared clones, beta-testing one of the ride systems. It was faster than revising the CAD simulations. Debra had a reputation for pursuing expedience.

"I'm starting to find out how it feels to work under pressure," I said, and nodded significantly at the Mansion. I was gratified to see him look embarrassed, then horrified.

"We would *never* touch the Mansion," he said. "It's *perfect*!"

Dan and Lil sauntered up as I was preparing a riposte. They both looked concerned—now that I thought of it, they'd both seemed incredibly concerned about me since the day I was revived.

Dan's gait was odd, stilted, like he was leaning on Lil for support. They looked like a couple. An irrational sear of jealousy jetted through me. I was an emotional wreck. Still, I took Lil's big, scarred hand in mine as soon as she was in reach, then cuddled her to me protectively. She had changed out of her maid's uniform into civvies: smart coveralls whose micropore fabric breathed in time with her own respiration.

"Lil, Dan, I want you to meet Tim Fung. He was just

telling me war stories from the Pirates project in Beijing."

Lil waved and Dan gravely shook his hand. "That was some hard work," Dan said.

It occurred to me to turn on some Whuffie monitors. It was normally an instantaneous reaction to meeting someone, but I was still disoriented. I pinged the elf. He had a lot of left-handed Whuffie; respect garnered from people who shared very few of my opinions. I expected that. What I didn't expect was that his weighted Whuffie score, the one that lent extra credence to the rankings of people I respected, was also high—higher than my own. I regretted my nonlinear behavior even more. Respect from the elf—*Tim,* I had to remember to call him Tim—would carry a lot of weight in every camp that mattered.

Dan's score was incrementing upwards, but he still had a rotten profile. He had accrued a good deal of left-handed Whuffie, and I curiously backtraced it to the occasion of my murder, when Debra's people had accorded him a generous dollop of props for the levelheaded way he had scraped up my corpse and moved it offstage, minimizing the disturbance in front of their wondrous Pirates.

I was fugueing, wandering off on the kind of mediated reverie that got me killed on the reef at Playa Coral, and I came out of it with a start, realizing that the other three were politely ignoring my blown buffer. I could have run backwards through my short-term memory to get the gist of the conversation, but that would have lengthened the pause. Screw it. "So, how're things going over at the Hall of the Presidents?" I asked Tim.

Lil shot me a cautioning look. She'd ceded the Hall to Debra's ad-hocs, that being the only way to avoid the appearance of childish disattention to the almighty Whuffie. Now she had to keep up the fiction of good-natured cooperation—that meant not shoulder-surfing Debra, looking for excuses to pounce on her work.

Tim gave us the same half-grin he'd greeted me with. On his smooth, pointed features, it looked almost irredeemably cute. "We're doing good stuff, I think. Debra's had her eye on the Hall for years, back in the old days, before she went to China. We're replacing the whole thing with broadband uplinks of gestalts from each of the Presidents' lives: newspaper headlines, speeches, distilled biographies, personal papers. It'll be like having each President *inside* you, core-dumped in a few seconds. Debra said we're going to *flash-bake* the Presidents on your mind!" His eyes glittered in the twilight.

Having only recently experienced my own cerebral flash-baking, Tim's description struck a chord in me. My personality seemed to be rattling around a little in my mind, as though it had been improperly fitted. It made the idea of having the gestalt of fifty-some Presidents squashed in along with it perversely appealing.

"Wow," I said. "That sounds wild. What do you have in mind for physical plant?" The Hall as it stood had a quiet, patriotic dignity cribbed from a hundred official buildings of the dead USA. Messing with it would be like redesigning the stars-and-bars.

"That's not really my area," Tim said. "I'm a programmer. But I could have one of the designers squirt some plans at you, if you want."

"That would be fine," Lil said, taking my elbow. "I think we should be heading home, now, though." She began to tug me away. Dan took my other elbow. Behind her, the Liberty Belle glowed like a ghostly wedding cake in the twilight.

"That's too bad," Tim said. "My ad-hoc is pulling an all-nighter on the new Hall. I'm sure they'd love to have you drop by."

The idea seized hold of me. I would go into the camp of the enemy, sit by their fire, learn their secrets. "That would be *great*!" I said, too loudly. My head was buzzing slightly. Lil's hands fell away.

"But we've got an early morning tomorrow," Lil said. "You've got a shift at eight, and I'm running into town for groceries." She was lying, but she was telling me that this wasn't her idea of a smart move. But my faith was unshakeable.

"Eight A.M. shift? No problem—I'll be right here when it starts. I'll just grab a shower at the Contemporary in the morning and catch the monorail back in time to change. All right?"

Dan tried. "But Jules, we were going to grab some dinner at Cinderella's Royal Table, remember? I made reservations."

"Aw, we can eat any time," I said. "This is a hell of an opportunity."

"It sure is," Dan said, giving up. "Mind if I come along?"

He and Lil traded meaningful looks that I interpreted to mean, *If he's going to be a nut, one of us really should stay with him.* I was past caring—I was going to beard the lion in his den!

Tim was apparently oblivious to all of this. "Then it's settled! Let's go."

On the walk to the Hall, Dan kept ringing my cochlea and I kept sending him straight to voicemail. All the while, I kept up a patter of small talk with him and Tim. I was determined to make up for my debacle in the Mansion with Tim, win him over.

Debra's people were sitting around in the armchairs onstage, the animatronic presidents stacked in neat piles in the wings. Debra was sprawled in Lincoln's armchair, her head cocked lazily, her legs extended before her. The Hall's normal smells of ozone and cleanliness were overridden by sweat and machine oil, the stink of an ad-hoc pulling an all-nighter. The Hall took fifteen years to research and execute, and a couple of days to tear down.

She was au naturel, still wearing the face she'd been born with, albeit one that had been regenerated dozens of times after her deaths. It was patrician, waxy, long, with a nose that was made for staring down. She was at least as old as I was, though she was only apparent twenty-two. I got the sense that she picked this age because it was one that afforded boundless reserves of energy.

She didn't deign to rise as I approached, but she did nod languorously at me. The other ad-hocs had been split into little clusters, hunched over terminals. They all had the raccoon-eyed, sleep-deprived look of fanatics, even Debra, who managed to look lazy and excited simultaneously.

Did you have me killed? I wondered, staring at Debra. After all, she'd been killed dozens, if not hundreds of times. It might not be such a big deal for her.

"Hi there," I said, brightly. "Tim offered to show us around! You know Dan, right?"

Debra nodded at him. "Oh, sure. Dan and I are pals, right?"

Dan's poker face didn't twitch a muscle. "Hello, Debra," he said. He'd been hanging out with them since Lil had briefed him on the peril to the Mansion, trying to gather some intelligence for us to use. They knew what he was up to, of course, but Dan was a fairly charming guy and he worked like a mule, so they tolerated him. But it seemed like he'd violated a boundary by accompanying me, as though the polite fiction that he was more a part of Debra's ad-hoc than Lil's was shattered by my presence.

Tim said, "Can I show them the demo, Debra?"

Debra quirked an eyebrow, then said, "Sure, why not. You'll like this, guys."

Tim hustled us backstage, where Lil and I used to sweat over the animatronics and cop surreptitious feels. Everything had been torn loose, packed up, stacked. They hadn't wasted a moment—they'd spent a week tearing down a show that had run for more than a century. The scrim that the projected portions of the show normally screened on was ground into the floor, spotted with grime, footprints and oil.

Tim showed me to a half-assembled backup terminal. Its housing was off, and any number of wireless keyboards, pointers and gloves lay strewn about. It had the look of a prototype.

"This is it—our uplink. So far, we've got a demo app running on it: Lincoln's old speech, along with the civil war montage. Just switch on guest access and I'll core-dump it to you. It's wild."

I pulled up my HUD and switched on guest access. Tim pointed a finger at the terminal and my brain was suffused with the essence of Lincoln: every nuance of his speech, the painstakingly researched movement tics, his warts and beard and topcoat. It almost felt like I *was* Lincoln, for a moment, and then it passed. But I could still taste the lingering coppery flavor of cannon-fire and chewing tobacco.

I staggered backwards. My head swam with flash-baked sense-impressions, rich and detailed. I knew on the spot that Debra's Hall of the Presidents was going to be a hit.

Dan took a shot off the uplink, too. Tim and I watched him as his expression shifted from skepticism to delight. Tim looked expectantly at me.

"That's really fine," I said. "Really, really fine. Moving."

Tim blushed. "Thanks! I did the gestalt programming—it's my specialty."

Debra spoke up from behind him—she'd sauntered over while Dan was getting his jolt. "I got the idea in Beijing, when I was dying a lot. There's something wonderful about having memories implanted, like you're really working your brain. I love the synthetic clarity of it all."

Tim sniffed. "Not synthetic at all," he said, turning to me. "It's nice and soft, right?"

I sensed deep political shoals and was composing my reply when Debra said: "Tim keeps trying to make it all more impressionistic, less computer-y. He's wrong, of course. We don't want to simulate the experience of watching the show—we want to *transcend* it."

Tim nodded reluctantly. "Sure, transcend it. But the way we do that is by making the experience *human,* a mile in the Presidents' shoes. Empathy-driven. What's the point of flash-baking a bunch of dry facts on someone's brain?"

One night in the Hall of Presidents convinced me of three things:

1. That Debra's people had had me killed, and screw their alibis.

2. That they would kill me again, when the time came for them to make a play for the Haunted Mansion.

3. That our only hope for saving the Mansion was a preemptive strike against them: we had to hit them hard, where it hurt.

Dan and I had been treated to eight hours of insectile precision in the Hall of Presidents, Debra's people working with effortless cooperation born of the adversity they'd faced in Beijing. Debra moved from team to team, making suggestions with body language as much as with words, leaving bursts of inspired activity in her wake.

It was that precision that convinced me of point one. Any ad-hoc this tight could pull off anything if it advanced their agenda. Ad-hoc? Hell, call them what they were: an army.

Point two came to me when I sampled the Lincoln build that Tim finished at about three in the morning, after intensive consultation with Debra. The mark of a great ride is that it gets better the second time around, as the detail and flourishes start to impinge on your consciousness. The Mansion was full of little gimcracks and sly nods that snuck into your experience on each successive ride.

Tim shuffled his feet nervously, bursting with barely restrained pride as I switched on public access. He dumped the app to my public directory, and, gingerly, I executed it.

God! God and Lincoln and cannon-fire and oratory and ploughs and mules and greatcoats! It rolled over me, it punched through me, it crashed against the inside of my skull and rebounded. The first pass through, there had been a sense of order, of narrative, but this, this was gestalt, the whole thing in one undifferentiated ball, filling me and spilling over. It was panicky for a moment, as the essence of Lincolness seemed to threaten my own personality, and, just as it was about to overwhelm me, it receded, leaving behind a rush of endorphin and adrenaline that made me want to jump.

"Tim," I gasped. "Tim! That was . . ." Words failed me. I wanted to hug him. What we could do for the Mansion with this! What elegance! Directly imprinting the experience, without recourse to the stupid, blind eyes; the thick, deaf ears.

Tim beamed and basked, and Debra nodded solemnly from her throne. "You liked it?" Tim said. I nodded, and staggered back to the theatre seat where Dan slept, head thrown back, snores softly rattling in his throat.

Incrementally, reason trickled back into my mind, and with it came ire. How dare they? The wonderful compromises of technology and expense that had given us the Disney rides—rides that had entertained the world for a century and more—could never compete head to head with what they were working on.

My hands knotted into fists in my lap. Why the fuck couldn't they do this somewhere else? Why did they have to destroy everything I loved to realize this? They could build this tech anywhere—they could distribute it online and people could access it from their living rooms!

But that would never do. Doing it here was better for the old Whuffie—they'd make over Disney World and hold it, a single ad-hoc where three hundred had flourished before, smoothly operating a park twice the size of Manhattan.

I stood and stalked out of the theater, out into Liberty Square and the Park. It had cooled down without drying out, and there was a damp chill that crawled up my back and made my breath stick in my throat.

I turned to contemplate the Hall of Presidents, staid and solid as it had been since my boyhood and before, a monument to the Imagineers who anticipated the Bitchun Society, inspired it.

I called Dan, still snoring back in the theater, and woke him. He grunted unintelligibly in my cochlea.

"They did it—they killed me." I knew they had, and I was glad. It made what I had to do next easier.

"Oh, Jesus. They didn't kill you—they offered their backups, remember? They couldn't have done it."

"Bullshit!" I shouted into the empty night. "Bullshit! They did it, and they fucked with their backups somehow. They must have. It's all too neat and tidy. How else could they have gotten so far with the Hall so fast? They knew it was coming, they planned a disruption, and they moved in. Tell me that you think they just had these plans lying around and moved on them when they could."

Dan groaned, and I heard his joints popping. He must have been stretching. The Park breathed around me, the sounds of maintenance crews scurrying in the night. "I do believe that. Clearly, you don't. It's not the first time we've disagreed. So now what?"

"Now we save the Mansion," I said. "Now we fight back."

"Oh, shit," Dan said.

I have to admit, there was a part of me that concurred.

• • •

My opportunity came later that week. Debra's ad-hocs were showboating, announcing a special preview of the new Hall to the other ad-hocs that worked in the Park. It was classic chutzpah, letting the key influencers in the Park in long before the bugs were hammered out. A smooth run would garner the kind of impressed reaction that guaranteed continued support while they finished up; a failed demo could doom them. There were plenty of people in the Park who had a sentimental attachment to the Hall of Presidents, and whatever Debra's people came up with would have to answer their longing.

"I'm going to do it during the demo," I told Dan, while I piloted the runabout from home to the cast-member parking. I snuck a look at him to gauge his reaction. He had his poker face on.

"I'm not going to tell Lil," I continued. "It's better that she doesn't know—plausible deniability."

"And me?" he said. "Don't I need plausible deniability?"

"No," I said. "No, you don't. You're an outsider. You can make the case that you were working on your own—gone rogue." I knew it wasn't fair. Dan was here to build up his Whuffie, and if he was implicated in my dirty scheme, he'd have to start over again. I knew it wasn't fair, but I didn't care. I knew that we were fighting for our own survival. "It's good versus evil, Dan. You don't want to be a post-person. You want to stay human. The rides are human. We each mediate them through our own experience. We're physically inside of them, and they talk to us through our senses. What Debra's people are building—it's hive-mind shit. Directly implanting thoughts! Jesus! It's not an experience, it's brainwashing! You gotta know that." I was pleading, arguing with myself as much as with him.

I snuck another look at him as I sped along the Disney backroads, lined with sweaty Florida pines and immaculate purple signage. Dan was looking thoughtful, the way he had back in our old days in Toronto. Some of my tension dissipated. He was thinking about it—I'd gotten through to him.

"Jules, this isn't one of your better ideas." My chest tightened, and he patted my shoulder. He had the knack of putting me at my ease, even when he was telling me that I was an idiot. "Even if Debra was behind your assassination—and that's not a certainty, we both know that. Even if that's the case, we've got better means at our disposal. Improving the Mansion, competing with her head to head, that's smart. Give it a little while and we can come back at her, take over the Hall—even the Pirates, that'd really piss her off. Hell, if we can prove she was behind the assassination, we can chase her off right now. Sabotage is not going to do you any good. You've got lots of other options."

"But none of them are fast enough, and none of them are emotionally satisfying. This way has some goddamn *balls*."

We reached castmember parking, I swung the runabout into a slot and stalked out before it had a chance to extrude its recharger cock. I heard Dan's door slam behind me and knew that he was following behind.

We took to the utilidors grimly. I walked past the cameras, knowing that my image was being archived, my presence logged. I'd picked the timing of my raid carefully: by arriving at high noon, I was sticking to my traditional pattern for watching hot-weather crowd dynamics. I'd made a point of visiting twice during the previous week at this time, and of dawdling in the commissary before heading topside. The delay between my arrival in the runabout and my showing up at the Mansion would not be discrepant.

Dan dogged my heels as I swung towards the commissary, and then hugged the wall, in the camera's blindspot. Back in my early days in the Park, when I was courting Lil, she showed me the A-Vac, the old pneumatic waste disposal system, decommissioned in the twenties. The kids who grew up in the Park had been notorious explorers of the tubes, which still whiffed faintly of the garbage bags they'd once whisked at 60-mph to the dump on the property's outskirts; but for a brave, limber kid, the tubes were a subterranean wonderland to explore when the hypermediated experiences of the Park lost their luster.

I snarled a grin and popped open the service entrance. "If they hadn't killed me and forced me to switch to a new body, I probably wouldn't be flexible enough to fit in," I hissed at Dan. "Ironic, huh?"

I clambered inside without waiting for a reply, and started inching my way under the Hall of Presidents.

My plan had covered every conceivable detail, except one, which didn't occur to me until I was forty minutes into the pneumatic tube, arms held before me and legs angled back like a swimmer's.

How was I going to reach into my pockets?

Specifically, how was I going to retrieve my HERF gun from my back pants pocket, when I couldn't even bend my elbows? The HERF gun was the crux of the plan: a High Energy Radio Frequency generator with a directional, focused beam that would punch up through the floor of the Hall of Presidents and fuse every goddamn scrap of unshielded electronics on the premises. I'd gotten the germ of the idea during Tim's first demo, when I'd seen all of his prototypes spread out backstage, cases off, ready to be tinkered with. Unshielded.

"Dan," I said, my voice oddly muffled by the tube's walls.

"Yeah?" he said. He'd been silent during the journey, the sound of his painful, elbow-dragging progress through the lightless tube my only indicator of his presence.

"Can you reach my back pocket?"

"Oh, shit," he said.

"Goddamn it," I said, "keep the fucking editorial to yourself. Can you reach it or not?"

I heard him grunt as he pulled himself up in the tube, then felt his hand groping up my calf. Soon, his chest was crushing my calves into the tube's floor and his hand was pawing around my ass.

"I can reach it," he said. I could tell from his tone that he wasn't too happy about my snapping at him, but I was too wrapped up to consider an apology, despite what must be happening to my Whuffie as Dan did his slow burn.

He fumbled the gun—a narrow cylinder as long as my palm—out of my pocket. "Now what?" he said.

"Can you pass it up?" I asked.

Dan crawled higher, overtop of me, but stuck fast when his ribcage met my glutes. "I can't get any further," he said.

"Fine," I said. "You'll have to fire it, then." I held my breath. Would he do it? It was one thing to be my accomplice, another to be the author of the destruction.

"Aw, Jules," he said.

"A simple yes or no, Dan. That's all I want to hear from you." I was boiling with anger—at myself, at Dan, at Debra, at the whole goddamn thing.

"Fine," he said.

"Good. Dial it up to max dispersion and point it straight up."

I heard him release the catch, felt a staticky crackle

in the air, and then it was done. The gun was a one-shot, something I'd confiscated from a mischievous guest a decade before, when they'd had a brief vogue.

"Hang on to it," I said. I had no intention of leaving such a damning bit of evidence behind. I resumed my bellycrawl forward to the next service hatch, near the parking lot, where I'd stashed an identical change of clothes for both of us.

We made it back just as the demo was getting underway. Debra's ad-hocs were ranged around the mezzanine inside the Hall of Presidents, a collection of influential castmembers from other ad-hocs filling the pre-show area to capacity.

Dan and I filed in just as Tim was stringing the velvet rope up behind the crowd. He gave me a genuine smile and shook my hand, and I smiled back, full of good feelings now that I knew that he was going down in flames. I found Lil and slipped my hand into hers as we filed into the auditorium, which had the new-car smell of rug shampoo and fresh electronics.

We took our seats and I bounced my leg nervously, compulsively, while Debra, dressed in Lincoln's coat and stovepipe, delivered a short speech. There was some kind of broadcast rig mounted over the stage now, something to allow them to beam us all their app in one humongous burst.

Debra finished up and stepped off the stage to a polite round of applause, and they started the demo.

Nothing happened. I tried to keep the shit-eating grin off my face as nothing happened. No tone in my cochlea indicating a new file in my public directory, no rush of sensation, nothing. I turned to Lil to make some snotty remark, but her eyes were closed, her mouth lolling open, her breath coming in short huffs. Down the row, every castmember was in the same attitude of deep, mind-blown concentration. I pulled up a diagnostic HUD.

Nothing. No diagnostics. No HUD. I cold-rebooted.

Nothing.

I was offline.

Offline, I filed out of the Hall of Presidents. Offline, I took Lil's hand and walked to the Liberty Belle loadzone, our spot for private conversations. Offline, I bummed a cigarette from her.

Lil was upset—even through my bemused, offline haze, I could tell that. Tears pricked her eyes.

"Why didn't you tell me?" she said, after a hard moment's staring into the moonlight reflecting off the river.

"Tell you?" I said, dumbly.

"They're really good. They're better than good. They're better than us. Oh, God."

Offline, I couldn't find stats or signals to help me discuss the matter. Offline, I tried it without help. "I don't think so. I don't think they've got soul, I don't think they've got history, I don't think they've got any kind of connection to the past. The world grew up in the Disneys—they visit this place for continuity as much as for entertainment. We provide that." I'm offline, and they're not—what the hell happened?

"It'll be OK, Lil. There's nothing in that place that's better than us. Different and new, but not better. You know that—you've spent more time in the Mansion than anyone, you know how much refinement, how much work there is in there. How can something they whipped up in a couple weeks possibly be better than this thing we've been maintaining for all these years?"

She ground the back of her sleeve against her eyes and smiled. "Sorry," she said. Her nose was red, her eyes puffy, her freckles livid over the flush of her cheeks. "Sorry—it's just shocking. Maybe you're right. And even if you're not—hey, that's the whole point of a meritocracy, right? The best stuff survives, everything else gets supplanted.

"Oh, shit, I hate how I look when I cry," she said. "Let's go congratulate them."

As I took her hand, I was obscurely pleased with myself for having improved her mood without artificial assistance.

Dan was nowhere to be seen as Lil and I mounted the stage at the Hall, where Debra's ad-hocs and a knot of well-wishers were celebrating by passing a rock around. Debra had lost the tailcoat and hat, and was in an extreme state of relaxation, arms around the shoulders of two of her cronies, pipe between her teeth.

She grinned around the pipe as Lil and I stumbled through some insincere compliments, nodded, and toked heavily while Tim applied a torch to the bowl.

"Thanks," she said, laconically. "It was a team effort." She hugged her cronies to her, almost knocking their heads together.

Lil said, "What's your timeline, then?"

Debra started unreeling a long spiel about critical paths, milestones, requirements meetings, and I tuned her out. Ad-hocs were crazy for that process stuff. I stared at my feet, at the floorboards, and realized that they weren't floorboards at all, but faux-finish painted over a copper mesh—a Faraday cage. That's why the HERF gun hadn't done anything; that's why they'd been so casual about working with the shielding off their computers. With my eye, I followed the copper shielding around the entire stage and up the walls, where it disappeared into the ceiling. Once again, I was struck by the evolvedness of Debra's ad-hocs, how their trial by fire in China had armored them against the kind of bush-league jiggery-pokery that the fuzzy bunnies in Florida—myself included—came up with.

For instance, I didn't think there was a single cast-member in the Park outside of Deb's clique with the stones to stage an assassination. Once I'd made that leap, I realized that it was only a matter of time until they staged another one—and another, and another. Whatever they could get away with.

Debra's spiel finally wound down and Lil and I headed away. I stopped in front of the backup terminal in the gateway between Liberty Square and Fantasyland. "When was the last time you backed up?" I asked her. If they could go after me, they might go after any of us.

"Yesterday," she said. She exuded bone-weariness at me, looking more like an overmediated guest than a tireless castmember.

"Let's run another backup, huh? We should really back up at night and at lunchtime—with things the way they are, we can't afford to lose an afternoon's work, much less a week's."

Lil rolled her eyes. I knew better than to argue with her when she was tired, but this was too crucial to set aside for petulance. "You can back up that often if you want to, Julius, but don't tell me how to live my life, OK?"

"Come on, Lil—it only takes a minute, and it'd make me feel a lot better. Please?" I hated the whine in my voice.

"No, Julius. No. Let's go home and get some sleep. I want to do some work on new merch for the Mansion—some collectible stuff, maybe."

"For Christ's sake, is it really so much to ask? Fine. Wait while I back up, then, all right?"

Lil groaned and glared at me.

I approached the terminal and cued a backup. Nothing happened. Oh, yeah, right, I was offline. A cool sweat broke out all over my new body.

• • •

Lil grabbed the couch as soon as we got in, mumbling something about wanting to work on some revised merch ideas she'd had. I glared at her as she subvocalized and air-typed in the corner, shut away from me. I hadn't told her that I was offline yet—it just seemed like insignificant personal bitching relative to the crises she was coping with.

Besides, I'd been knocked offline before, though not in fifty years, and often as not the system righted itself after a good night's sleep. I could visit the doctor in the morning if things were still screwy.

So I crawled into bed, and when my bladder woke me in the night, I had to go into the kitchen to consult our old starburst clock to get the time. It was three A.M., and when the hell had we expunged the house of all timepieces, anyway?

Lil was sacked out on the couch, and complained feebly when I tried to rouse her, so I covered her with a blanket and went back to bed, alone.

I woke disoriented and crabby, without my customary morning jolt of endorphin. Vivid dreams of death and destruction slipped away as I sat up. I preferred to let my subconscious do its own thing, so I'd long ago programmed my systems to keep me asleep during REM cycles except in emergencies. The dream left a foul taste in my mind as I staggered into the kitchen, where Lil was fixing coffee.

"Why didn't you wake me up last night? I'm one big

ache from sleeping on the couch," Lil said as I stumbled in.

She had the perky, jaunty quality of someone who could instruct her nervous system to manufacture endorphin and adrenaline at will. I felt like punching the wall.

"You wouldn't get up," I said, and slopped coffee in the general direction of a mug, then scalded my tongue with it.

"And why are you up so late? I was hoping you would cover a shift for me—the merch ideas are really coming together and I wanted to hit the Imagineering shop and try some prototyping."

"Can't." I foraged a slice of bread with cheese and noticed a crumby plate in the sink. Dan had already eaten and gone, apparently.

"Really?" she said, and my blood started to boil in earnest. I slammed Dan's plate into the dishwasher and shoved bread into my maw.

"Yes. Really. It's your shift—fucking work it or call in sick."

Lil reeled. Normally, I was the soul of sweetness in the morning, when I was hormonally enhanced, anyway. "What's wrong, honey?" she said, going into helpful castmember mode. Now I wanted to hit something besides the wall.

"Just leave me alone, all right? Go fiddle with fucking merch. I've got real work to do—in case you haven't noticed, Debra's about to eat you and your little band of plucky adventurers and pick her teeth with the bones. For God's sake, Lil, don't you ever get fucking angry about anything? Don't you have any goddamned passion?"

Lil whitened and I felt a sinking feeling in my gut. It was the worst thing I could possibly have said.

Lil and I had met three years before, at a barbecue that some friends of her parents threw, a kind of cast-member mixer. She'd been just nineteen then—apparent and real—and had a bubbly, flirty vibe that made me dismiss her, at first, as just another airhead cast-member.

Her parents—Tom and Rita—on the other hand, were fascinating people, members of the original ad-hoc that had seized power in Walt Disney World, wresting control from a gang of wealthy former shareholders who'd been operating it as their private preserve. Rita was apparent twenty or so, but she radiated a maturity and a fiery devotion to the Park that threw her daughter's superficiality into sharp relief.

They throbbed with Whuffie, Whuffie beyond measure, beyond use. In a world where even a zeroed-out Whuffie loser could eat, sleep, travel and access the net without hassle, their wealth was more than sufficient to repeatedly access the piffling few scarce things left on earth over and over.

The conversation turned to the first day, when she and her pals had used a cutting torch on the turnstiles and poured in, wearing homemade costumes and name tags. They infiltrated the shops, the control centers, the rides, first by the hundred, then, as the hot

July day ticked by, by the thousand. The shareholders' lackeys—who worked the Park for the chance to be a part of the magic, even if they had no control over the management decisions—put up a token resistance. Before the day was out, though, the majority had thrown in their lots with the raiders, handing over security codes and pitching in.

"But we knew the shareholders wouldn't give in as easy as that," Lil's mother said, sipping her lemonade. "We kept the Park running twenty-four seven for the next two weeks, never giving the shareholders a chance to fight back without doing it in front of the guests. We'd prearranged with a couple of airline adhocs to add extra routes to Orlando, and the guests came pouring in." She smiled, remembering the moment, and her features in repose were Lil's almost identically. It was only when she was talking that her face changed, muscles tugging it into an expression decades older than the face that bore it.

"I spent most of the time running the merch stand at Madame Leota's outside the Mansion, gladhanding the guests while hissing nasties back and forth with the shareholders who kept trying to shove me out. I slept in a sleeping bag on the floor of the utilidor, with a couple dozen others, in three hour shifts. That was when I met this asshole"—she chucked her husband on the shoulder—"he'd gotten the wrong sleeping bag by mistake and wouldn't budge when I came down to crash. I just crawled in next to him and the rest, as they say, is history."

Lil rolled her eyes and made gagging noises. "Jesus, Rita, no one needs to hear about that part of it."

Tom patted her arm. "Lil, you're an adult—if you can't stomach hearing about your parents' courtship, you can either sit somewhere else or grin and bear it. But you don't get to dictate the topic of conversation."

Lil gave us adults a very youthful glare and flounced off. Rita shook her head at Lil's departing backside. "There's not much fire in that generation," she said. "Not a lot of passion. It's our fault—we thought that Disney World would be the best place to raise a child in the Bitchun Society. Maybe it was, but . . ." She trailed off and rubbed her palms on her thighs, a gesture I'd come to know in Lil, by and by. "I guess there aren't enough challenges for them these days. They're too cooperative." She laughed and her husband took her hand.

"We sound like our parents," Tom said. " 'When we were growing up, we didn't have any of this newfangled life-extension stuff—we took our chances with the cave bears and the dinosaurs!' " Tom wore himself older, apparent fifty, with graying sidewalls and crinkled smile-lines, the better to present a non-threatening air of authority to the guests. It was a truism among the first-gen ad-hocs that women cast-members should wear themselves young, men old. "We're just a couple of Bitchun fundamentalists, I guess."

Lil called over from a nearby conversation: "Are they telling you what a pack of milksops we are, Julius? When you get tired of that, why don't you come over here and have a smoke?" I noticed that she and her cohort were passing a crack pipe.

"What's the use?" Lil's mother sighed.

"Oh, I don't know that it's as bad as all that," I said, virtually my first words of the afternoon. I was painfully conscious that I was only there by courtesy, just one of the legion of hopefuls who flocked to Orlando every year, aspiring to a place among the ruling cliques. "They're passionate about maintaining the Park, that's for sure. I made the mistake of lifting a queue-gate at the Jungleboat Cruise last week and I got a very earnest lecture about the smooth functioning of the Park from a castmember who couldn't have been more than eighteen. I think that they don't have the passion for creating Bitchunry that we have—they don't need it—but they've got plenty of drive to maintain it."

Lil's mother gave me a long, considering look that I didn't know what to make of. I couldn't tell if I had offended her or what.

"I mean, you can't be a revolutionary after the revolution, can you? Didn't we all struggle so that kids like Lil wouldn't have to?"

"Funny you should say that," Tom said. He had the same considering look on his face. "Just yesterday we were talking about the very same thing. We were talking—" he drew a breath and looked askance at his wife, who nodded—"about deadheading. For a while, anyway. See if things changed much in fifty or a hundred years."

I felt a kind of shameful disappointment. Why was I wasting my time schmoozing with these two, when they wouldn't be around when the time came to vote me in? I banished the thought as quickly as it came—I was talking to them because they were nice people. Not every conversation had to be strategically important.

"Really? Deadheading." I remember that I thought of Dan then, about his views on the cowardice of deadheading, on the bravery of ending it when you found yourself obsolete. He'd comforted me once, when my last living relative, my uncle, opted to go to sleep for three thousand years. My uncle had been born pre-Bitchun, and had never quite gotten the hang of it. Still, he was my link to my family, to my first adulthood and my only childhood. Dan had taken me to Ganonoque and we'd spent the day bounding around the countryside on seven-league boots, sailing high over the lakes of the Thousand Islands and the crazy fiery carpet of autumn leaves. We topped off the day at a dairy commune he knew where they still made cheese from cow's milk and there'd been a thousand smells and bottles of strong cider and a girl whose name I'd long since forgotten but whose exuberant laugh I'd remember forever. And it wasn't so important, then, my uncle going to sleep for three millennia, because whatever happened, there were the leaves and the lakes and the crisp sunset the color of blood and the girl's laugh.

"Have you talked to Lil about it?"

Rita shook her head. "It's just a thought, really. We don't want to worry her. She's not good with hard decisions—it's her generation."

They changed the subject not long thereafter, and I sensed discomfort, knew that they had told me too much, more than they'd intended. I drifted off and found Lil and her young pals, and we toked a little and cuddled a little.

Within a month, I was working at the Haunted Mansion, Tom and Rita were invested in Canopic jars in Kissimmee with instructions not to be woken until their newsbots grabbed sufficient interesting material to make it worth their while, and Lil and I were a hot item.

Lil didn't deal well with her parents' decision to deadhead. For her, it was a slap in the face, a reproach to her and her generation of twittering Polyannic cast-members.

For God's sake, Lil, don't you ever get fucking angry about anything? Don't you have any goddamned passion?

The words were out of my mouth before I knew I was saying them, and Lil, fifteen percent of my age, young enough to be my great-granddaughter; Lil, my lover and best friend and sponsor to the Liberty Square ad-hocracy; Lil turned white as a sheet, turned on her heel and walked out of the kitchen. She got in her runabout and went to the Park to take her shift.

I went back to bed and stared at the ceiling fan as it made its lazy turns, and felt like shit.

Five

When I finally returned to the Park, 36 hours had passed and Lil had not come back to the house. If she'd tried to call, she would've gotten my voicemail—I had no way of answering my phone. As it turned out, she hadn't been trying to reach me at all.

I'd spent the time alternately moping, drinking, and plotting terrible, irrational vengeance on Debra for killing me, destroying my relationship, taking away my beloved (in hindsight, anyway) Hall of Presidents and threatening the Mansion. Even in my addled state, I knew that this was pretty unproductive, and I kept promising that I would cut it out, take a shower and some sober-ups, and get to work at the Mansion.

I was working up the energy to do just that when Dan came in.

"Jesus," he said, shocked. I guess I was a bit of a mess, sprawled on the sofa in my underwear, all gamy and baggy and bloodshot.

"Hey, Dan. How's it goin'?"

He gave me one of his patented wry looks and I felt the same weird reversal of roles that we'd undergone at the U of T, when he had become the native, and I had become the interloper. He was the together one with the wry looks and I was the pathetic seeker who'd burned all his reputation capital. Out of habit, I checked my Whuffie, and a moment later I stopped being startled by its low score and was instead shocked by the fact that I could check it at all. I was back online!

"Now, what do you know about that?" I said, staring at my dismal Whuffie.

"What?" he said.

I called his cochlea. "My systems are back online," I subvocalized.

He started. "You were offline?"

I jumped up from the couch and did a little happy underwear dance. "I *was,* but I'm not *now.*" I felt better than I had in days, ready to beat the world—or at least Debra.

"Let me take a shower, then let's get to the Imagineering labs. I've got a pretty kickass idea."

The idea, as I explained it in the runabout, was a preemptive rehab of the Mansion. Sabotaging the Hall had been a nasty, stupid idea, and I'd gotten what I deserved for it. The whole point of the Bitchun Society was to be more reputable than the next ad-hoc, to succeed on merit, not trickery, despite assassinations and the like.

So a rehab it would be.

"Back in the early days of the Disneyland Mansion, in California," I explained, "They had a guy in a suit of armor just past the first Doom Buggy curve; he'd leap out and scare the hell out of the guests as they went by. It didn't last long, of course. The poor bastard kept getting punched out by startled guests, and besides, the armor wasn't too comfortable for long shifts."

Dan chuckled appreciatively. The Bitchun Society had all but done away with any sort of dull, repetitious labor, and what remained—tending bar, mopping toilets—commanded Whuffie aplenty and a life of leisure in your off-hours.

"But that guy in the suit of armor, he could *improvise*. You'd get a slightly different show every time. It's like the castmembers who spiel on the Jungleboat Cruise. They've each got their own patter, their own jokes, and even though the animatronics aren't so hot, it makes the show worth seeing."

"You're going to fill the Mansion with castmembers in armor?" Dan asked, shaking his head.

I waved away his objections, causing the runabout to swerve, terrifying a pack of guests who were taking a ride on rented bikes around the property. "No," I said, flapping a hand apologetically at the white-faced guests. "Not at all. But what if all of the animatronics had human operators—telecontrollers, working with waldoes? We'll let them interact with the guests, talk with them, scare them . . . We'll get rid of the existing animatronics, replace 'em with full-mobility robots, then cast the parts over the Net. Think of the Whuffie! You could put, say, a thousand operators online at once, ten shifts per day, each of them caught up in our Mansion. We'll give out awards for outstanding performances, the shifts'll be based on popular vote. In effect, we'll be adding another ten thousand guests to the Mansion's throughput every day, only these guests will be honorary castmembers."

"That's pretty good," Dan said. "Very Bitchun. Debra may have AI and flash-baking, but you'll have human interaction, courtesy of the biggest Mansion-fans in the world—"

"And those are the very fans Debra'll have to win over to make a play for the Mansion. Very elegant, huh?"

The first order of business was to call Lil, patch things up, and pitch the idea to her. The only problem was, my cochlea was offline again. My mood started to sour, and I had Dan call her instead.

We met her up at Imagineering, a massive complex of prefab aluminum buildings painted Go-Away Green that had thronged with mad inventors since the Bitchun Society had come to Walt Disney World. The adhocs who had built an Imagineering department in

Florida and now ran the thing were the least political in the Park, classic labcoat-and-clipboard types who would work for anyone so long as the ideas were cool. Not caring about Whuffie meant that they accumulated it in plenty on both the left and right hands.

Lil was working with Suneep, AKA the Merch Miracle. He could design, prototype and produce a souvenir faster than anyone—shirts, sculptures, pens, toys, housewares, he was the king. They were collaborating on their HUDs, facing each other across a labbench in the middle of a lab as big as a basketball court, cluttered with logomarked tchotchkes and gabbling away while their eyes danced over invisible screens.

Dan reflexively joined the collaborative space as he entered the lab, leaving me the only one out on the joke. Dan was clearly delighted by what he saw.

I nudged him with an elbow. "Make a hard copy," I hissed.

Instead of pitying me, he just airtyped a few commands and pages started to roll out of a printer in the lab's corner. Anyone else would have made a big deal out of it, but he just brought me into the discussion.

If I needed proof that Lil and I were meant for each other, the designs she and Suneep had come up with were more than enough. She'd been thinking just the way I had—souvenirs that stressed the human scale of the Mansion. There were miniature animatronics of the Hitchhiking Ghosts in a black-light box, their skeletal robotics visible through their layers of plastic clothing; action figures that communicated by IR, so that placing one in proximity with another would unlock its Mansion-inspired behaviors—the raven cawed, Mme. Leota's head incanted, the singing busts sang. She'd worked up some formal attire based on the castmember costume, cut in this year's stylish lines.

It was good merch, is what I'm trying to say. In my mind's eye, I was seeing the relaunch of the Mansion in six months, filled with robotic avatars of Mansion-nuts the world round, Mme. Leota's gift cart piled high with brilliant swag, strolling human players ad-libbing with the guests in the queue area. . . .

Lil looked up from her mediated state and glared at me as I pored over the hardcopy, nodding enthusiastically.

"Passionate enough for you?" she snapped.

I felt a flush creeping into my face, my ears. It was somewhere between anger and shame, and I reminded myself that I was more than a century older than her, and it was my responsibility to be mature. Also, I'd started the fight.

"This is fucking fantastic, Lil," I said. Her look didn't soften. "Really choice stuff. I had a great idea—" I ran it down for her, the avatars, the robots, the rehab. She stopped glaring, started taking notes, smiling, showing me her dimples, her slanted eyes crinkling at the corners.

"This isn't easy," she said, finally. Suneep, who'd been politely pretending not to listen in, nodded involuntarily. Dan, too.

"I know that," I said. The flush burned hotter. "But that's the point—what Debra does isn't easy either. It's risky, dangerous. It made her and her ad-hoc better—it made them sharper." *Sharper than us, that's for sure.* "They can make decisions like this fast, and execute them just as quickly. We need to be able to do that, too."

Was I really advocating being more like Debra? The words'd just popped out, but I saw that I'd been right—we'd have to beat Debra at her own game, outevolve her ad-hocs.

"I understand what you're saying," Lil said. I could tell she was upset—she'd reverted to castmember-speak. "It's a very good idea. I think that we stand a good chance of making it happen if we approach the group and put it to them, after doing the research, building the plans, laying out the critical path, and privately soliciting feedback from some of them."

I felt like I was swimming in molasses. At the rate that the Liberty Square ad-hoc moved, we'd be holding formal requirements reviews while Debra's people tore down the Mansion around us. So I tried a different tactic.

"Suneep, you've been involved in some rehabs, right?"

Suneep nodded slowly, with a cautious expression,

a nonpolitical animal being drawn into a political discussion.

"OK, so tell me, if we came to you with this plan and asked you to pull together a production schedule—one that didn't have any review, just take the idea and run with it—and then pull it off, how long would it take you to execute it?"

Lil smiled primly. She'd dealt with Imagineering before.

"About five years," he said, almost instantly.

"Five years?" I squawked. "Why five years? Debra's people overhauled the Hall in a month!"

"Oh, wait," he said. "No review at all?"

"No review. Just come up with the best way you can to do this, and do it. And we can provide you with unlimited, skilled labor, three shifts around the clock."

He rolled his eyes back and ticked off days on his fingers while muttering under his breath. He was a tall, thin man with a shock of curly dark hair that he smoothed unconsciously with surprisingly stubby fingers while he thought.

"About eight weeks," he said. "Barring accidents, assuming off-the-shelf parts, unlimited labor, capable management, material availability . . ." He trailed off again, and his short fingers waggled as he pulled up a HUD and started making a list.

"Wait," Lil said, alarmed. "How do you get from five years to eight weeks?"

Now it was my turn to smirk. I'd seen how Imagineering worked when they were on their own, building prototypes and conceptual mockups—I knew that the real bottleneck was the constant review and revisions, the ever-fluctuating groupmind consensus of the ad-hoc that commissioned their work.

Suneep looked sheepish. "Well, if all I have to do is satisfy myself that my plans are good and my buildings won't fall down, I can make it happen very fast. Of course, my plans aren't perfect. Sometimes, I'll be halfway through a project when someone suggests a new flourish or approach that makes the whole thing immeasurably better. Then it's back to the drawing board. . . . So I stay at the drawing board for a long time at the start, get feedback from other Imagineers, from the ad-hocs, from focus groups and the Net. Then we do reviews at every stage of construction, check to see if anyone has had a great idea we haven't thought of and incorporate it, sometimes rolling back the work.

"It's slow, but it works."

Lil was flustered. "But if you can do a complete revision in eight weeks, why not just finish it, then plan another revision, do *that* one in eight weeks, and so on? Why take five years before anyone can ride the thing?"

"Because that's how it's done," I said to Lil. "But that's not how it *has* to be done. That's how we'll save the Mansion."

I felt the surety inside of me, the certain knowledge that I was right. Ad-hocracy was a great thing, a Bitchun thing, but the organization needed to turn on a dime—that would be even *more* Bitchun.

"Lil," I said, looking into her eyes, trying to burn my POV into her. "We have to do this. It's our only chance. We'll recruit hundreds to come to Florida and work on the rehab. We'll give every Mansion nut on the planet a shot at joining up, then we'll recruit them again to work at it, to run the telepresence rigs. We'll get buy-in from the biggest super-recommenders in the world, and we'll build something better and faster than any ad-hoc ever has, without abandoning the original Imagineers' vision. It will be unspeakably Bitchun."

Lil dropped her eyes, and it was her turn to flush. She paced the floor, hands swinging at her sides. I could tell that she was still angry with me, but excited and scared and yes, passionate.

"It's not up to me, you know," she said at length, still pacing. Dan and I exchanged wicked grins. She was in.

"I know," I said. But it was, almost—she was a real opinion-leader in the Liberty Square ad-hoc, someone who knew the systems back and forth, someone who made good, reasonable decisions and kept her head in a crisis. Not a hothead. Not prone to taking radical switchbacks. This plan would burn up that reputation and the Whuffie that accompanied it in short order, but by the time that happened, she'd have plenty of Whuffie with the new, thousands-strong ad-hoc.

"I mean, I can't guarantee anything. I'd like to study

the plans that Imagineering comes through with, do some walk-throughs—"

I started to object, to remind her that speed was of the essence, but she beat me to it.

"But I won't. We have to move fast. I'm in."

She didn't come into my arms, didn't kiss me and tell me everything was forgiven, but she bought in, and that was enough.

My systems came back online sometime that day, and I hardly noticed, I was so preoccupied with the new Mansion. Holy shit, was it ever audacious: since the first Mansion opened in California in 1969, no one had ever had the guts to seriously fuxor with it. Oh, sure, the Paris version, Phantom Manor, had a slightly different storyline, but it was just a minor bit of tweakage to satisfy the European market at the time. No one wanted to screw up the legend.

What the hell made the Mansion so cool, anyway? I'd been to Disney World any number of times as a guest before I settled in, and truth be told, it had never been my absolute favorite.

But when I returned to Disney World, live and in person, freshly bored stupid by the three-hour live-headed flight from Toronto, I'd found myself crowd-driven to it.

I'm a terrible, terrible person to visit theme parks with. Since I was a punk kid snaking my way through crowded subway platforms, eeling into the only seat on a packed car, I'd been obsessed with Beating The Crowd.

In the early days of the Bitchun Society, I'd known a blackjack player, a compulsive counter of cards, an idiot savant of odds. He was a pudgy, unassuming engineer, the moderately successful founder of a moderately successful high-tech startup that had done something arcane with software agents. While he was only moderately successful, he was fabulously wealthy: he'd never raised a cent of financing for his company, and had owned it outright when he finally sold it for a bathtub full of money. His secret was the green felt tables of Vegas, where he'd pilgrim off to every time his bank balance dropped, there to count the monkey-cards and calculate the odds and Beat The House.

Long after his software company was sold, long after he'd made his nut, he was dressing up in silly disguises and hitting the tables, grinding out hand after hand of twenty-one, for the sheer satisfaction of Beating The House. For him, it was pure brain-reward, a jolt of happy-juice every time the dealer busted and every time he doubled down on a deckfull of face cards.

Though I'd never bought so much as a lottery ticket, I immediately got his compulsion: for me, it was Beating The Crowd, finding the path of least resistance, filling the gaps, guessing the short queue, dodging the traffic, changing lanes with a whisper to spare—moving with precision and grace and, above all, *expedience.*

On that fateful return, I checked into the Fort Wilderness Campground, pitched my tent, and fairly ran to the ferry docks to catch a barge over to the Main Gate.

Crowds were light until I got right up to Main Gate and the ticketing queues. Suppressing an initial instinct to dash for the farthest one, beating my ferry-mates to what rule-of-thumb said would have the shortest wait, I stepped back and did a quick visual survey of the twenty kiosks and evaluated the queued-up huddle in front of each. Pre-Bitchun, I'd have been primarily interested in their ages, but that is less and less a measure of anything other than outlook, so instead I carefully examined their queuing styles, their dress, and more than anything, their burdens.

You can tell more about someone's ability to efficiently negotiate the complexities of a queue through what they carry than through any other means—if only more people realized it. The classic, of course, is the unladen citizen, a person naked of even a modest shoulderbag or marsupial pocket. To the layperson, such a specimen might be thought of as a sure bet for a fast transaction, but I'd done an informal study and come to the conclusion that these brave iconoclasts are often the flightiest of the lot, left smiling with bovine mystification, patting down their pockets in a fruitless search for a writing implement, a piece of ID, a keycard, a rabbit's foot, a rosary, a tuna sandwich.

No, for my money, I'll take what I call the Road Worrier anytime. Such a person is apt to be carefully slung with four or five carriers of one description or another, from bulging cargo pockets to clever military-grade strap-on pouches with biometrically keyed closures. The thing to watch for is the ergonomic consideration given to these conveyances: do they balance, are they slung for minimum interference and maximum ease of access? Someone who's given that much consideration to their gear is likely spending his time in line determining which bits and pieces he'll need when he reaches its headwaters, and is holding them at the ready for fastest-possible processing.

This is a tricky call, since there are lookalike pretenders, gear-pigs who pack *everything* because they lack the organizational smarts to figure out what they should pack—they're just as apt to be burdened with bags and pockets and pouches, but the telltale is the efficiency of that slinging. These pack mules will sag beneath their loads, juggling this and that while pushing overloose straps up on their shoulders.

I spied a queue that was made up of a group of Road Worriers, a queue that was slightly longer than the others, but I joined it and ticced nervously as I watched my progress relative to the other spots I could've chosen. I was borne out, a positive omen for a wait-free World, and I was sauntering down Main Street, USA long before my ferrymates.

Returning to Walt Disney World was a homecoming

for me. My parents had brought me the first time when I was all of ten, just as the first inklings of the Bitchun society were trickling into everyone's consciousness: the death of scarcity, the death of death, the struggle to rejig an economy that had grown up focused on nothing but scarcity and death. My memories of the trip are dim but warm, the balmy Florida climate and a sea of smiling faces punctuated by magical, darkened moments riding in OmniMover cars, past diorama after diorama.

I went again when I graduated high school and was amazed by the richness of detail, the grandiosity and grandeur of it all. I spent a week there stunned bovine, grinning and wandering from corner to corner. Someday, I knew, I'd come to live there.

The Park became a touchstone for me, a constant in a world where everything changed. Again and again, I came back to the Park, grounding myself, communing with all the people I'd been.

That day I bopped from land to land, ride to ride, seeking out the short lines, the eye of the hurricane that crowded the Park to capacity. I'd take high ground, standing on a bench or hopping up on a fence, and do a visual reccy of all the queues in sight, try to spot prevailing currents in the flow of the crowd, generally having a high old obsessive time. Truth be told, I probably spent as much time looking for walk-ins as I would've spent lining up like a good little sheep, but I had more fun and got more exercise.

The Haunted Mansion was experiencing a major

empty spell: the Snow Crash Spectacular parade had just swept through Liberty Square en route to Fantasyland, dragging hordes of guests along with it, dancing to the JapRap sounds of the comical Sushi-K and aping the movements of the brave Hiro Protagonist. When they blew out, Liberty Square was a ghost town, and I grabbed the opportunity to ride the Mansion five times in a row, walking on every time.

The way I tell it to Lil, I noticed her and then I noticed the Mansion, but to tell the truth it was the other way around.

The first couple rides through, I was just glad of the aggressive air conditioning and the delicious sensation of sweat drying on my skin. But on the third pass, I started to notice just how goddamn cool the thing was. There wasn't a single bit of tech more advanced than a film-loop projector in the whole place, but it was all so cunningly contrived that the illusion of a haunted house was perfect: the ghosts that whirled through the ballroom were *ghosts,* three-dimensional and ethereal and phantasmic. The ghosts that sang in comical tableaux through the graveyard were equally convincing, genuinely witty and simultaneously creepy.

My fourth pass through, I noticed the *detail,* the hostile eyes worked into the wallpaper's pattern, the motif repeated in the molding, the chandeliers, the photo gallery. I began to pick out the words to "Grim Grinning Ghosts," the song that is repeated throughout the ride, whether in sinister organ-tones repeating the main theme *troppo troppo* or the spritely singing of the four musical busts in the graveyard.

It's a catchy tune, one that I hummed on my fifth pass through, this time noticing that the over-aggressive AC was, actually, mysterious chills that blew through the rooms as wandering spirits made their presence felt. By the time I debarked for the fifth time, I was whistling the tune with jazzy improvisations in a mixed-up tempo.

That's when Lil and I ran into each other. She was picking up a discarded ice cream wrapper—I'd seen a dozen castmembers picking up trash that day, seen it so frequently that I'd started doing it myself. She grinned slyly at me as I debarked into the fried-food-and-disinfectant perfume of the Park, hands in pockets, thoroughly pleased with myself for having so completely *experienced* a really fine hunk of art.

I smiled back at her, because it was only natural that one of the Whuffie-kings who were privileged to tend this bit of heavenly entertainment should notice how thoroughly I was enjoying her work.

"That's really, really Bitchun," I said to her, admiring the titanic mountains of Whuffie my HUD attributed to her.

She was in character, and not supposed to be cheerful, but castmembers of her generation can't help but be friendly. She compromised between ghastly demeanor and her natural sweet spirit, and leered a grin at me, thumped through a zombie's curtsey, and moaned "Thank you—we *do* try to keep it *spirited.*"

I groaned appreciatively, and started to notice just how very cute she was, this little button of a girl with her rotting maid's uniform and her feather-shedding duster. She was just so clean and scrubbed and happy about everything, she radiated it and made me want to pinch her cheeks—either set.

The moment was on me, and so I said, "When do they let you ghouls off? I'd love to take you out for a Zombie or a Bloody Mary."

Which led to more horrifying banter, and to my taking her out for a couple at the Adventurer's Club, learning her age in the process and losing my nerve, telling myself that there was nothing we could possibly have to say to each other across a century-wide gap.

While I tell Lil that I noticed her first and the Mansion second, the reverse is indeed true. But it's also true—and I never told her this—that the thing I love best about the Mansion is:

It's where I met her.

Dan and I spent the day riding the Mansion, drafting scripts for the telepresence players who we hoped to bring onboard. We were in a totally creative zone, the dialog running as fast as he could transcribe it. Jamming on ideas with Dan was just about as terrific as a pastime could be.

I was all for leaking the plan to the Net right away, getting hearts-and-minds action with our core audience, but Lil turned it down.

She was going to spend the next couple days quietly politicking among the rest of the ad-hoc, getting some support for the idea, and she didn't want the appearance of impropriety that would come from having outsiders being brought in before the ad-hoc.

Talking to the ad-hocs, bringing them around—it was a skill I'd never really mastered. Dan was good at it, Lil was good at it, but me, I think that I was too self-centered to ever develop good skills as a peacemaker. In my younger days, I assumed that it was because I was smarter than everyone else, with no patience for explaining things in short words for mouth-breathers who just didn't get it.

The truth of the matter is, I'm a bright enough guy, but I'm hardly a genius. Especially when it comes to people. Probably comes from Beating The Crowd, never seeing individuals, just the mass—the enemy of expedience.

I never would have made it into the Liberty Square ad-hoc on my own. Lil made it happen for me, long before we started sleeping together. I'd assumed that her folks would be my best allies in the process of joining up, but they were too jaded, too ready to take the long sleep to pay much attention to a newcomer like me.

Lil took me under her wing, inviting me to after-work parties, talking me up to her cronies, quietly passing around copies of my thesis work. And she did the same in reverse, sincerely extolling the virtues of the others I met, so that I knew what there was to respect about them and couldn't help but treat them as individuals. In the years since, I'd lost that respect. Mostly, I palled around with Lil, and once he arrived, Dan, and with net-friends around the world. The ad-hocs that I worked with all day treated me with basic courtesy but not much friendliness.

I guess I treated them the same. When I pictured them in my mind, they were a faceless, passive-aggressive mass, too caught up in the starchy world of consensus-building to ever do much of anything.

Dan and I threw ourselves into it headlong, trolling the Net for address lists of Mansion-otakus from the four corners of the globe, spreadsheeting them against their timezones, temperaments, and, of course, their Whuffie.

"That's weird," I said, looking up from the old-fashioned terminal I was using—my systems were back offline. They'd been sputtering up and down for a couple days now, and I kept meaning to go to the doctor, but I'd never gotten round to it. Periodically, I'd get a jolt of urgency when I remembered that this meant my backup was stale-dating, but the Mansion always took precedence.

"Huh?" he said.

I tapped the display. "See these?" It was a fan-site, displaying a collection of animated 3-D meshes of various elements of the Mansion, part of a giant collaborative project that had been ongoing for decades, to build an accurate 3-D walkthrough of every inch of the Park. I'd used those meshes to build my own testing fly-throughs.

"Those are terrific," Dan said. "That guy must be a total *fiend.*" The meshes' author had painstakingly modeled, chained and animated every ghost in the ballroom scene, complete with the kinematics necessary for full motion. Where a "normal" fan-artist might've used a standard human kinematics library for the figures, this one had actually written his own from the ground up, so that the ghosts moved with a spectral fluidity that was utterly unhuman.

"Who's the author?" Dan asked. "Do we have him on our list yet?"

I scrolled down to display the credits. "I'll be damned," Dan breathed.

The author was Tim, Debra's elfin crony. He'd submitted the designs a week before my assassination.

"What do you think it means?" I asked Dan, though I had a couple ideas on the subject myself.

"Tim's a Mansion nut," Dan said. "I knew that."

"You knew?"

He looked a little defensive. "Sure. I told you, back when you had me hanging out with Debra's gang."

Had I asked him to hang out with Debra? As I remembered it, it had been his suggestion. Too much to think about.

"But what does it mean, Dan? Is he an ally? Should

we try to recruit him? Or is he the one that'd convinced Debra she needs to take over the Mansion?"

Dan shook his head. "I'm not even sure that she wants to take over the Mansion. I know Debra; all she wants to do is turn ideas into things, as fast and as copiously as possible. She picks her projects carefully. She's acquisitive, sure, but she's cautious. She had a great idea for Presidents, and so she took over. I never heard her talk about the Mansion."

"Of course you didn't. She's cagey. Did you hear her talk about the Hall of Presidents?"

Dan fumbled. "Not really . . . I mean, not in so many words, but—"

"But nothing," I said. "She's after the Mansion, she's after the Magic Kingdom, she's after the Park. She's taking over, goddamn it, and I'm the only one who seems to have noticed."

I came clean to Lil about my systems that night, as we were fighting. Fighting had become our regular evening pastime, and Dan had taken to sleeping at one of the hotels on-site rather than endure it.

I'd started it, of course. "We're going to get killed if we don't get off our asses and start the rehab," I said, slamming myself down on the sofa and kicking at the scratched coffee table. I heard the hysteria and unreason in my voice and it just made me madder. I was frustrated by not being able to check in on Suneep and

Dan, and, as usual, it was too late at night to call anyone and do anything about it. By the morning, I'd have forgotten again.

From the kitchen, Lil barked back, "I'm doing what I can, Jules. If you've got a better way, I'd love to hear about it."

"Oh, bullshit. I'm doing what I can, planning the thing out. I'm ready to *go*. It was your job to get the ad-hocs ready for it, but you keep telling me they're not. When will they be?"

"Jesus, you're a nag."

"I wouldn't nag if you'd only fucking make it happen. What are you doing all day, anyway? Working shifts at the Mansion? Rearranging deck chairs on the Great Titanic Adventure?"

"I'm working my fucking *ass* off. I've spoken to every goddamn one of them at least twice this week about it."

"Sure," I hollered at the kitchen. "Sure you have."

"Don't take my word for it, then. Check my fucking phone logs."

She waited.

"Well? Check them!"

"I'll check them later," I said, dreading where this was going.

"Oh, no you *don't*." she said, stalking into the room, fuming. "You can't call me a liar and then refuse to look at the evidence." She planted her hands on her slim little hips and glared at me. She'd gone pale and

I could count every freckle on her face, her throat, her collarbones, the swell of her cleavage in the old vee-neck shirt I'd given her on a day-trip to Nassau.

"Well?" she asked. She looked ready to wring my neck.

"I can't," I admitted, not meeting her eyes.

"Yes you can—here, I'll dump it to your public directory."

Her expression shifted to one of puzzlement when she failed to locate me on her network. "What's going on?"

So I told her. Offline, outcast, malfunctioning.

"Well, why haven't you gone to the doctor? I mean, it's been *weeks*. I'll call him right now."

"Forget it," I said. "I'll see him tomorrow. No sense in getting him out of bed."

But I didn't see him the day after, or the day after that. Too much to do, and the only times I remembered to call someone, I was too far from a public terminal or it was too late or too early. My systems came online a couple times, and I was too busy with the plans for the Mansion. Lil grew accustomed to the drifts of hard copy that littered the house, to printing out her annotations to my designs and leaving them on my favorite chair—to living like the cavemen of the information age had, surrounded by dead trees and ticking clocks. Being offline helped me focus. Focus is hardly the word for it—I obsessed. I sat in front of the terminal I'd brought home all day, every day, crunching plans, dictating voicemail. People who wanted to reach me had to haul ass out to the house, and *speak* to me.

I grew too obsessed to fight, and Dan moved back, and then it was my turn to take hotel rooms so that the rattle of my keyboard wouldn't keep him up nights. He and Lil were working a full-time campaign to recruit the ad-hoc to our cause, and I started to feel like we were finally in harmony, about to reach our goal.

I went home one afternoon clutching a sheaf of hard copy and burst into the living room, gabbling a mile-a-minute about a wrinkle on my original plan that would add a third walk-through segment to the ride, increasing the number of telepresence rigs we could use without decreasing throughput.

I was mid-babble when my systems came back online. The public chatter in the room sprang up on my HUD.

And then I'm going to tear off every stitch of clothing and jump you.

And then what?

I'm going to bang you till you limp.

Jesus. Lil, you are one rangy cowgirl.

My eyes closed, shutting out everything except for the glowing letters. Quickly, they vanished. I opened my eyes again, looking at Lil, who was flushed and distracted. Dan looked scared.

"What's going on, Dan?" I asked quietly. My heart hammered in my chest, but I felt calm and detached.

"Jules," he began, then gave up and looked at Lil.

Lil had, by that time, figured out that I was back online, that their secret messaging had been discovered.

"Having fun, Lil?" I asked.

Lil shook her head and glared at me. "Just go, Julius. I'll send your stuff to the hotel."

"You want me to go, huh? So you can bang him till he limps?"

"This is my house, Julius. I'm asking you to get out of it. I'll see you at work tomorrow—we're having a general ad-hoc meeting to vote on the rehab."

It was her house.

"Lil, Julius—" Dan began.

"This is between me and him," Lil said. "Stay out of it."

I dropped my papers—I wanted to throw them, but I dropped them, *flump,* and I turned on my heel and walked out, not bothering to close the door behind me.

Dan showed up at the hotel ten minutes after I did and rapped on my door. I was all-over numb as I opened the door. He had a bottle of tequila—*my* tequila, brought over from the house that I'd shared with Lil.

He sat down on the bed and stared at the logo-marked wallpaper. I took the bottle from him, got a couple glasses from the bathroom and poured.

"It's my fault," he said.

"I'm sure it is," I said.

"We got to drinking a couple nights ago. She was really upset. Hadn't seen you in days, and when she *did* see you, you freaked her out. Snapping at her. Arguing. Insulting her."

"So you made her," I said.

He shook his head, then nodded, took a drink. "I did. It's been a long time since I . . ."

"You had sex with my girlfriend, in my house, while I was away, working."

"Jules, I'm sorry. I did it, and I kept on doing it. I'm not much of a friend to either of you.

"She's pretty broken up. She wanted me to come out here and tell you it was all a mistake, that you were just being paranoid."

We sat in silence for a long time. I refilled his glass, then my own.

"I couldn't do that," he said. "I'm worried about you. You haven't been right, not for months. I don't know what it is, but you should get to a doctor."

"I don't need a doctor," I snapped. The liquor had melted the numbness and left burning anger and bile, my constant companions. "I need a friend who doesn't fuck my girlfriend when my back is turned."

I threw my glass at the wall. It bounced off, leaving tequila stains on the wallpaper, and rolled under the bed. Dan started, but stayed seated. If he'd stood up, I would've hit him. Dan's good at crises.

"If it's any consolation, I expect to be dead pretty

soon," he said. He gave me a wry grin. "My Whuffie's doing good. This rehab should take it up over the top. I'll be ready to go."

That stopped me. I'd somehow managed to forget that Dan, my good friend Dan, was going to kill himself.

"You're going to do it," I said, sitting down next to him. It hurt to think about it. I really liked the bastard. He might've been my best friend.

There was a knock at the door. I opened it without checking the peephole. It was Lil.

She looked younger than ever. Young and small and miserable. A snide remark died in my throat. I wanted to hold her.

She brushed past me and went to Dan, who squirmed out of her embrace.

"No," he said, and stood up and sat on the windowsill, staring down at the Seven Seas Lagoon.

"Dan's just been explaining to me that he plans on being dead in a couple months," I said. "Puts a damper on the long-term plans, doesn't it, Lil?"

Tears streamed down her face and she seemed to fold in on herself. "I'll take what I can get," she said.

I choked on a knob of misery, and I realized that it was Dan, not Lil, whose loss upset me the most.

Lil took Dan's hand and led him out of the room.

I guess I'll take what I can get, too, I thought.

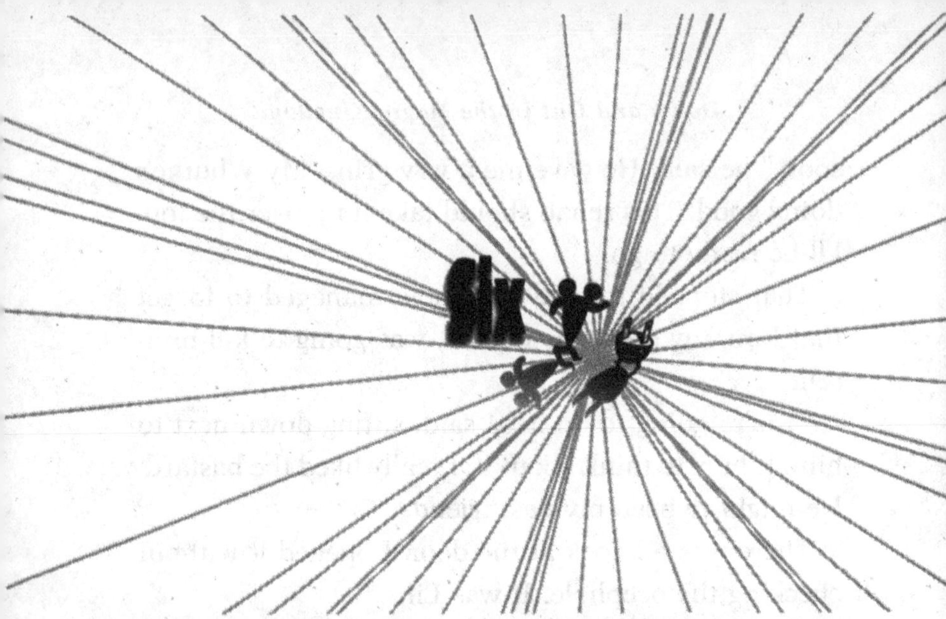

Lying on my hotel bed, mesmerized by the lazy turns of the ceiling fan, I pondered the possibility that I was nuts.

It wasn't unheard of, even in the days of the Bitchun Society, and even though there were cures, they weren't pleasant.

I was once married to a crazy person. We were both about seventy, and I was living for nothing but joy. Her name was Zoya, and I called her Zed.

We met in orbit, where I'd gone to experience the famèd low-gravity sybarites. Getting staggering drunk is not much fun at one gee, but at ten to the neg eight, it's a blast. You don't stagger, you *bounce.* and when you're bouncing in a sphere full of other bouncing, happy, boisterous naked people, things get deeply fun.

I was bouncing around inside a clear sphere that was a mile in diameter, filled with smaller spheres in which one could procure bulbs of fruity, deadly concoctions. Musical instruments littered the sphere's floor, and if you knew how to play, you'd snag one, tether it to you and start playing. Others would pick up their own axes and jam along. The tunes varied from terrific to awful, but they were always energetic.

I had been working on my third symphony on and off, and whenever I thought I had a nice bit nailed, I'd spend some time in the sphere playing it. Sometimes, the strangers who jammed in gave me new and interesting lines of inquiry, and that was good. Even when they didn't, playing an instrument was a fast track to intriguing an interesting, naked stranger.

Which is how we met. She snagged a piano and pounded out barrelhouse runs in quirky time as I carried the main thread of the movement on a cello. At first it was irritating, but after a short while I came to a dawning comprehension of what she was doing to my music, and it was really *good.* I'm a sucker for musicians.

We brought the session to a crashing stop, me bowing furiously as spheres of perspiration beaded on my body and floated gracefully into the hydrotropic recyclers, she beating on the eighty-eight like they were the perp who killed her partner.

I collapsed dramatically as the last note crashed through the bubble. The singles, couples and groups stopped in midflight coitus to applaud. She took a bow, untethered herself from the Steinway, and headed for the hatch.

I coiled my legs up and did a fast burn through the sphere, desperate to reach the hatch before she did. I caught her as she was leaving.

"Hey!" I said. "That was great! I'm Julius! How're you doing?"

She reached out with both hands and squeezed my nose and my unit simultaneously—not hard, you understand, but playfully. "Honk!" she said, and squirmed through the hatch while I gaped at my burgeoning chub-on.

I chased after her. "Wait," I called as she tumbled through the spoke of the station towards the gravity.

She had a pianist's body—re-engineered arms and hands that stretched for impossible lengths, and she used them with a spacehand's grace, vaulting herself forward at speed. I bumbled after her best as I could on my freshman spacelegs, but by the time I reached the half-gee rim of the station, she was gone.

I didn't find her again until the next movement was done and I went to the bubble to try it out on an oboe. I was just getting warmed up when she passed through the hatch and tied off to the piano.

This time, I clamped the oboe under my arm and bopped over to her before moistening the reed and blowing. I hovered over the piano's top, looking her in the eye as we jammed. Her mood that day was 4/4 time and I–IV–V progressions, in a feel that swung around from blues to rock to folk, teasing at the edge of my own melodies. She noodled at me, I noodled back at her, and her eyes crinkled charmingly whenever I managed a smidge of tuneful wit.

She was almost completely flat-chested, and covered in a fine, red downy fur, like a chipmunk. It was a jaunter's style, suited to the climate-controlled, soft-edged life in space. Fifty years later, I was dating Lil, another redhead, but Zed was my first.

I played and played, entranced by the fluidity of her movements at the keyboard, her comical moues of concentration when picking out a particularly kicky little riff. When I got tired, I took it to a slow bridge or gave her a solo. I was going to make this last as long as I could. Meanwhile, I maneuvered my way between her and the hatch.

When I blew the last note, I was wrung out as a washcloth, but I summoned the energy to zip over to the hatch and block it. She calmly untied and floated over to me.

I looked in her eyes, silvered slanted cat-eyes, eyes that I'd been staring into all afternoon, and watched the smile that started at their corners and spread right down to her long, elegant toes. She looked back at me, then, at length, grabbed ahold of my joint again.

"You'll do," she said, and led me to her sleeping quarters, across the station.

We didn't sleep.

Zoya had been an early network engineer for the geosynch broadband constellations that went up at the cusp of the world's ascent into Bitchunry. She'd been exposed to a lot of hard rads and low gee and had generally become pretty transhuman as time went by, upgrading with a bewildering array of third-party enhancements: a vestigial tail, eyes that saw through most of the RF spectrum, her arms, her fur, dogleg reversible knee joints and a completely mechanical spine that wasn't prone to any of the absolutely inane bullshit that plagues the rest of us, like lower-back pain, intrascapular inflammation, sciatica and slipped discs.

I thought I lived for fun, but I didn't have anything on Zed. She only talked when honking and whistling and grabbing and kissing wouldn't do, and routinely slapped upgrades into herself on the basis of any whim that crossed her mind, like when she resolved to do a spacewalk bare-skinned and spent the afternoon getting tin-plated and iron-lunged. I fell in love with her a hundred times a day, and wanted to strangle her twice as often. She stayed on her spacewalk for a couple of days, floating around the bubble, making crazy faces at its mirrored exterior. She had no way of knowing if I was inside, but she assumed that I was watching. Or maybe she didn't, and she was making faces for anyone's benefit.

But then she came back through the lock, strange and wordless and her eyes full of the stars she'd seen and her metallic skin cool with the breath of empty space, and she led me a merry game of tag through the station, the mess hall where we skidded sloppy through a wobbly ovoid of rice pudding, the greenhouses where she burrowed like a gopher and shinnied like a monkey, the living quarters and bubbles as we interrupted a thousand acts of coitus.

You'd have thought that we'd have followed it up with an act of our own, and truth be told, that was certainly my expectation when we started the game I came to think of as the steeplechase, but we never did. Halfway through, I'd lose track of carnal urges and return to a state of childlike innocence, living only for the thrill of the chase and the giggly feeling I got whenever she found some new, even-more-outrageous corner to turn. I think we became legendary on the station, that crazy pair that's always zipping in and zipping away, like having your party crashed by two naked, coed Marx Brothers.

When I asked her to marry me, to return to Earth with me, to live with me until the universe's mainspring unwound, she laughed, honked my nose and my willie and shouted, "YOU'LL *DO*!"

I took her home to Toronto and we took up residence ten stories underground in overflow residence for the University. Our Whuffie wasn't so hot earthside, and the endless institutional corridors made her feel at home while affording her opportunities for mischief.

But bit by bit, the mischief dwindled, and she started talking more. At first, I admit I was relieved, glad that my strange, silent wife was finally acting normal, making nice with the neighbors instead of pranking them with endless honks and fanny-kicks and squirt guns. We gave up the steeplechase and she had the doglegs taken out, her fur removed, her eyes unsilvered to a hazel that was pretty and as fathomable as the silver had been inscrutable.

We wore clothes. We entertained. I started to rehearse my symphony in low-Whuffie halls and parks with any musicians I could drum up, and she came out and didn't play, just sat to the side and smiled and smiled with a smile that never went beyond her lips.

She went nuts.

She shat herself. She pulled her hair. She cut herself with knives. She accused me of plotting to kill her. She set fire to the neighbors' apartments, wrapped herself in plastic sheeting, dry-humped the furniture.

She went nuts. She did it in broad strokes, painting the walls of our bedroom with her blood, jagging all night through rant after rant. I smiled and nodded and faced it for as long as I could, then I grabbed her and hauled her, kicking like a mule, to the doctor's office on the second floor. She'd been dirtside for a year and nuts for a month, but it took me that long to face up to it.

The doc diagnosed nonchemical dysfunction, which was by way of saying that it was her mind, not her brain, that was broken. In other words, I'd driven her nuts.

You can get counseling for nonchemical dysfunction, basically trying to talk it out, learn to feel better about yourself. She didn't want to.

She was miserable, suicidal, murderous. In the brief moments of lucidity that she had under sedation, she consented to being restored from a backup that was made before we came to Toronto.

I was at her side in the hospital when she woke up. I had prepared a written synopsis of the events since her last backup for her, and she read it over the next couple days.

"Julius," she said, while I was making breakfast in our subterranean apartment. She sounded so serious, so fun-free, that I knew immediately that the news wouldn't be good.

"Yes?" I said, setting out plates of bacon and eggs, steaming cups of coffee.

"I'm going to go back to space, and revert to an older version." She had a shoulderbag packed, and she had traveling clothes on.

Oh, shit. "Great," I said, with forced cheerfulness, making a mental inventory of my responsibilities dirtside. "Give me a minute or two, I'll pack up. I miss space, too."

She shook her head, and anger blazed in her utterly scrutable hazel eyes. "No. I'm going back to who I was, before I met you."

It hurt, bad. I had loved the old, steeplechase Zed, had loved her fun and mischief. The Zed she'd become after we wed was terrible and terrifying, but I'd stuck with her out of respect for the person she'd been.

Now she was off to restore herself from a backup made before she met me. She was going to lop eighteen months out of her life, start over again, revert to a saved version.

Hurt? It ached like a motherfucker.

I went back to the station a month later, and saw her jamming in the sphere with a guy who had three extra sets of arms depending from his hips. He scuttled around the sphere while she played a jig on the piano, and when her silver eyes lit on me, there wasn't a shred of recognition in them. She'd never met me.

I died some, too, putting the incident out of my head and sojourning to Disney World, there to reinvent myself with a new group of friends, a new career, a new life. I never spoke of Zed again—especially not to Lil, who hardly needed me to pollute her with remembrances of my crazy exes.

If I was nuts, it wasn't the kind of spectacular nuts that Zed had gone. It was a slow, seething, ugly nuts that had me alienating my friends, sabotaging my enemies, driving my girlfriend into my best friend's arms.

I decided that I would see a doctor, just as soon as we'd run the rehab past the ad-hoc's general meeting. I had to get my priorities straight.

I pulled on last night's clothes and walked out to the Monorail station in the main lobby. The platform was jammed with happy guests, bright and cheerful and ready for a day of steady, hypermediated fun. I tried to make myself attend to them as individuals, but try as I might, they kept turning into a crowd, and I had to plant my feet firmly on the platform to keep from weaving among them to the edge, the better to snag a seat.

The meeting was being held over the Sunshine Tree Terrace in Adventureland, just steps from where I'd been turned into a road-pizza by the still-unidentified assassin. The Adventureland ad-hocs owed the Liberty Square crew a favor since my death had gone down on their turf, so they had given us use of their prize meeting room, where the Florida sun streamed through the slats of the shutters, casting a hash of dust-filled shafts of light across the room. The faint sounds of the tiki-drums and the spieling Jungle Cruise guides leaked through the room, a low-key ambient buzz from two of the Park's oldest rides.

There were almost a hundred ad-hocs in the Liberty Square crew, almost all second-gen castmembers with big, friendly smiles. They filled the room to capacity, and there was much hugging and handshaking before the meeting came to order. I was thankful that the room was too small for the de rigeur ad-hoc circle-of-chairs, so that Lil was able to stand at a podium and command a smidge of respect.

"Hi there!" she said, brightly. The weepy puffiness was still present around her eyes, if you knew how to look for it, but she was expert at putting on a brave face no matter what the ache.

The ad-hocs roared back a collective, "Hi, Lil!" and laughed at their own corny tradition. Oh, they sure were a barrel of laughs at the Magic Kingdom.

"Everybody knows why we're here, right?" Lil said, with a self-deprecating smile. She'd been lobbying hard for weeks, after all. "Does anyone have any questions about the plans? We'd like to start executing right away."

A guy with deliberately boyish, wholesome features put his arm in the air. Lil acknowledged him with a nod. "When you say 'right away,' do you mean—"

I cut in. "Tonight. After this meeting. We're on an eight-week production schedule, and the sooner we start, the sooner it'll be finished."

The crowd murmured, unsettled. Lil shot me a withering look. I shrugged. Politics was not my game.

Lil said, "Don, we're trying something new here, a really streamlined process. The good part is, the process is *short*. In a couple months, we'll know if it's working for us. If it's not, hey, we can turn it around in a couple months, too. That's why we're not spending as much time planning as we usually do. It won't take five years for the idea to prove out, so the risks are lower."

Another castmember, a woman, apparent forty with a round, motherly demeanor said, "I'm all for moving fast—Lord knows, our pacing hasn't always been that hot. But I'm concerned about all these new people you propose to recruit—won't having more people slow us down when it comes to making new decisions?"

No, I thought sourly, *because the people I'm bringing in aren't addicted to meetings.*

Lil nodded. "That's a good point, Lisa. The offer

we're making to the telepresence players is probationary—they don't get to vote until after we've agreed that the rehab is a success."

Another castmember stood. I recognized him: Dave, a heavyset, self-important jerk who loved to work the front door, even though he blew his spiel about half the time. "Lillian," he said, smiling sadly at her, "I think you're really making a big mistake here. We love the Mansion, all of us, and so do the guests. It's a piece of history, and we're its custodians, not its masters. Changing it like this, well . . ." he shook his head. "It's not good stewardship. If the guests wanted to walk through a funhouse with guys jumping out of the shadows saying 'booga-booga,' they'd go to one of the Halloween Houses in their hometowns. The Mansion's better than that. I can't be a part of this plan."

I wanted to knock the smug grin off his face. I'd delivered essentially the same polemic a thousand times—in reference to Debra's work—and hearing it from this jerk in reference to *mine* made me go all hot and red inside.

"Look," I said. "If we don't do this, if we don't change things, they'll get changed *for* us. By someone else. The question, *Dave,* is whether a responsible custodian lets his custodianship be taken away from him, or whether he does everything he can to make sure that he's still around to ensure that his charge is properly cared for. Good custodianship isn't sticking your head in the sand."

I could tell I wasn't doing any good. The mood of

the crowd was getting darker, the faces more set. I resolved not to speak again until the meeting was done, no matter what the provocation.

Lil smoothed my remarks over, and fielded a dozen more, and it looked like the objections would continue all afternoon and all night and all the next day, and I felt woozy and overwrought and miserable all at the same time, staring at Lil and her harried smile and her nervous smoothing of her hair over her ears.

Finally, she called the question. By tradition, the votes were collected in secret and publicly tabulated over the data-channels. The group's eyes unfocussed as they called up HUDs and watched the totals as they rolled in. I was offline and unable to vote or watch.

At length, Lil heaved a relieved sigh and smiled, dropping her hands behind her back.

"All right then," she said, over the crowd's buzz. "Let's get to work."

I stood up, saw Dan and Lil staring into each other's eyes, a meaningful glance between new lovers, and I saw red. Literally. My vision washed over pink, and a strobe pounded at the edges of my vision. I took two lumbering steps towards them and opened my mouth to say something horrible, and what came out was "Waaagh." My right side went numb and my leg slipped out from under me and I crashed to the floor.

The slatted light from the shutters cast its way across my chest as I tried to struggle up with my left arm, and then it all went black.

• • •

I wasn't nuts after all.

The doctor's office in the Main Street infirmary was clean and white and decorated with posters of Jiminy Cricket in doctors' whites with an outsized stethoscope. I came to on a hard pallet under a sign that reminded me to get a check-up twice a year, by gum! and I tried to bring my hands up to shield my eyes from the over-bright light and the over-cheerful signage, and discovered that I couldn't move my arms. Further investigation revealed that this was because I was strapped down, in full-on four-point restraint.

"Waaagh," I said again.

Dan's worried face swam into my field of vision, along with a serious-looking doctor, apparent seventy, with a Norman Rockwell face full of crow's-feet and smile-lines.

"Welcome back, Julius. I'm Doctor Pete," the doctor said, in a kindly voice that matched the face. Despite my recent disillusion with castmember bullshit, I found his schtick comforting.

I slumped back against the palette while the doc shone lights in my eyes and consulted various diagnostic apparatus. I bore it in stoic silence, too confounded by the horrible Waaagh sounds to attempt more speech. The doc would tell me what was going on when he was ready.

"Does he need to be tied up still?" Dan asked, and I shook my head urgently. Being tied up wasn't my idea of a good time.

The doc smiled kindly. "I think it's for the best, for

now. Don't worry, Julius, we'll have you up and about soon enough."

Dan protested, but stopped when the doc threatened to send him out of the room. He took my hand instead.

My nose itched. I tried to ignore it, but it got worse and worse, until it was all I could think of, the flaming lance of itch that strobed at the tip of my nostril. Furiously, I wrinkled my face, rattled at my restraints. The doc absentmindedly noticed my gyrations and delicately scratched my nose with a gloved finger. The relief was fantastic. I just hoped my nuts didn't start itching anytime soon.

Finally, the doctor pulled up a chair and did something that caused the head of the bed to raise up so that I could look him in the eye.

"Well, now," he said, stroking his chin. "Julius, you've got a problem. You friend here tells me your systems have been offline for more than a month. It sure would've been better if you'd come in to see me when it started up.

"But you didn't, and things got worse." He nodded up at Jiminy Cricket's recriminations: Go ahead, see your doc! "It's good advice, son, but what's done is done. You were restored from a backup about eight weeks ago, I see. Without more tests, I can't be sure, but my theory is that the brain-machine interface they installed at that time had a material defect. It's been deteriorating ever since, misfiring and rebooting. The shut-downs are a protective mechanism, meant to keep it from introducing the kind of seizure you experienced this afternoon. When the interface senses malfunction, it shuts itself down and boots a diagnostic mode, attempts to fix itself and come back online.

"Well, that's fine for minor problems, but in cases like this, it's bad news. The interface has been deteriorating steadily, and it's only a matter of time before it does some serious damage."

"Waaagh?" I asked. I meant to say, *All right, but what's wrong with my mouth?*

The doc put a finger to my lips. "Don't try. The interface has locked up, and it's taken some of your voluntary nervous processes with it. In time, it'll probably shut down, but for now, there's no point. That's why we've got you strapped down—you were thrashing pretty hard when they brought you in, and we didn't want you to hurt yourself."

Probably shut down? Jesus. I could end up stuck like this forever. I started shaking.

The doc soothed me, stroking my hand, and in the process pressed a transdermal on my wrist. The panic receded as the transdermal's sedative oozed into my bloodstream.

"There, there," he said. "It's nothing permanent. We can grow you a new clone and refresh it from your last backup. Unfortunately, that backup is a few months old. If we'd caught it earlier, we may've been able to salvage a current backup, but given the deterioration you've displayed to date . . . Well, there just wouldn't be any point."

My heart hammered. I was going to lose two months—lose it all, never happened. My assassination, the new Hall of Presidents and my shameful attempt thereon, the fights with Lil, Lil and Dan, the meeting. My plans for the rehab! All of it, good and bad, every moment flensed away.

I couldn't do it. I had a rehab to finish, and I was the only one who understood how it had to be done. Without my relentless prodding, the ad-hocs would surely revert to their old, safe ways. They might even leave it half-done, halt the process for an interminable review, present soft belly for Debra to savage.

I wouldn't be restoring from backup.

I had two more seizures before the interface finally gave up and shut itself down. I remember the first, a confusion of vision-occluding strobes and uncontrollable thrashing and the taste of copper, but the second happened without waking me from deep unconsciousness.

When I came to again in the infirmary, Dan was still there. He had a day's growth of beard and new worry-lines at the corners of his newly rejuvenated eyes. The doctor came in, shaking his head.

"Well, now, it seems like the worst is over. I've drawn up the consent forms for the refresh and the new clone will be ready in an hour or two. In the meantime, I think heavy sedation is in order. Once the restore's been completed, we'll retire this body for you and we'll be all finished up."

Retire this body? Kill me, is what it meant.

"No," I said. I thrilled in my restraints: my voice was back under my control!

"Oh, really now." The doc lost his bedside manner, let his exasperation slip through. "There's nothing else for it. If you'd come to me when it all started, well, we might've had other options. You've got no one to blame but yourself."

"No," I repeated. "Not now. I won't sign."

Dan put his hand on mine. I tried to jerk out from under it, but the restraints and his grip held me fast. "You've got to do it, Julius. It's for the best," he said.

"I'm not going to let you kill me," I said, through clenched teeth. His fingertips were callused, worked rough with exertion well beyond the normal call of duty.

"No one's killing you, son," the doctor said. Son, son, son. Who knew how old he was? He could be eighteen for all I knew. "It's just the opposite: we're saving you. If you continue like this, it will only get worse. The seizures, mental breakdown, the whole melon going soft. You don't want that."

I thought of Zed's spectacular transformation into a crazy person. *No, I sure don't.* "I don't care about the interface. Chop it out. I can't do it now." I swallowed. "Later. After the rehab. Eight more weeks."

• • •

The irony! Once the doc knew I was serious, he sent Dan out of the room and rolled his eyes up while he placed a call. I saw his gorge work as he subvocalized. He left me bound to the table, to wait.

No clocks in the infirmary, and no internal clock, and it may have been ten minutes or five hours. I was catheterized, but I didn't know it until urgent necessity made the discovery for me.

When the doc came back, he held a small device that I instantly recognized: a HERF gun.

Oh, it wasn't the same model I'd used on the Hall of Presidents. This one was smaller, and better made, with the precise engineering of a surgical tool. The doc raised his eyebrows at me. "You know what this is," he said, flatly. A dim corner of my mind gibbered, *he knows, he knows, the Hall of Presidents.* But he didn't know. That episode was locked in my mind, invulnerable to backup.

"I know," I said.

"This one is high-powered in the extreme. It will penetrate the interface's shielding and fuse it. It probably won't turn you into a vegetable. That's the best I can do. If this fails, we will restore you from your last backup. You have to sign the consent before I use it." He'd dropped all kindly pretense from his voice, not bothering to disguise his disgust. I was pitching out the miracle of the Bitchun Society, the thing that had all but obsoleted the medical profession: why bother with surgery when you can grow a clone, take a backup, and refresh the new body? Some people swapped corpuses just to get rid of a cold.

I signed. The doc wheeled my gurney into the crash and hum of the utilidors and then put it on a freight tram that ran to the Imagineering compound, and thence to a heavy, exposed Faraday cage. Of course: using the HERF on me would kill any electronics in the neighborhood. They had to shield me before they pulled the trigger.

The doc placed the gun on my chest and loosened my restraints. He sealed the cage and retreated to the lab's door. He pulled a heavy apron and helmet with faceguard from a hook beside the door.

"Once I am outside the door, point it at your head and pull the trigger. I'll come back in five minutes. Once I am in the room, place the gun on the floor and do not touch it. It is only good for a single usage, but I have no desire to find out I'm wrong."

He closed the door. I took the pistol in my hand. It was heavy, dense with its stored energy, the tip a parabolic hollow to better focus its cone.

I lifted the gun to my temple and let it rest there. My thumb found the trigger-stud.

I paused. This wouldn't kill me, but it might lock the interface forever, paralyzing me, turning me into a thrashing maniac. I knew that I would never be able to pull the trigger. The doc must've known, too—this was his way of convincing me to let him do that restore.

I opened my mouth to call the doc, and what came out was "Waaagh!"

The seizure started. My arm jerked and my thumb nailed the stud, and there was an ozone tang. The seizure stopped.

I had no more interface.

The doc looked sour and pinched when he saw me sitting up on the gurney, rubbing at my biceps. He produced a handheld diagnostic tool and pointed it at my melon, then pronounced every bit of digital microcircuitry in it dead. For the first time since my twenties, I was no more advanced than nature had made me.

The restraints had left purple bruises at my wrists and ankles where I'd thrashed against them. I hobbled out of the Faraday cage and the lab under my own power, but just barely, my muscles groaning from the inadvertent isometric exercises of my seizures.

Dan was waiting in the utilidor, crouched and dozing against the wall. The doc shook him awake and his head snapped up, his hand catching the doc's in a lightning-quick reflex. It was easy to forget Dan's old line of work here in the Magic Kingdom, but when he smoothly snagged the doc's arm and sprang to his feet, eyes hard and alert, I remembered. My old pal, the action hero.

Quickly, Dan released the doc and apologized. He assessed my physical state and wordlessly wedged his shoulder in my armpit, supporting me. I didn't have the strength to stop him. I needed sleep.

"I'm taking you home," he said. "We'll fight Debra off tomorrow."

"Sure," I said, and boarded the waiting tram.

But we didn't go home. Dan took me back to my hotel, the Contemporary, and brought me up to my door. He keycarded the lock and stood awkwardly as I hobbled into the empty room that was my new home, as I collapsed into the bed that was mine now.

With an apologetic look, he slunk away, back to Lil and the house we'd shared.

I slapped on a sedative transdermal that the doc had given me, and added a mood-equalizer that he'd recommended to control my "personality swings." In seconds, I was asleep.

The meds helped me cope with the next couple of days, starting the rehab on the Mansion. We worked all night erecting a scaffolding around the facade, though no real work would be done on it—we wanted the appearance of rapid progress, and besides, I had an idea.

I worked alongside Dan, using him as a personal secretary, handling my calls, looking up plans, monitoring the Net for the first grumblings as the Disney-going public realized that the Mansion was being taken down for a full-blown rehab. We didn't exchange any unnecessary words, standing side by side without ever looking into one another's eyes. I couldn't really feel awkward around Dan, anyway. He never let me, and besides we had our hands full directing disappointed guests away from the Mansion. A depressing number of them headed straight for the Hall of Presidents.

We didn't have to wait long for the first panicked screed about the Mansion to appear. Dan read it aloud off his HUD: "Hey! Anyone hear anything about scheduled maintenance at the HM? I just buzzed by on the way to the new H of P's and it looks like some big stuff's afoot—scaffolding, castmembers swarming in and out, see the pic. I hope they're not screwing up a good thing. BTW, don't miss the new H of P's—very Bitchun."

"Right," I said. "Who's the author, and is he on the list?"

Dan cogitated a moment. "*She* is Kim Wright, and she's on the list. Good Whuffie, lots of Mansion fanac, big readership."

"Call her," I said.

This was the plan: recruit rabid fans right away, get 'em in costume, and put 'em up on the scaffolds. Give them outsized, bat-adorned tools and get them to play at construction activity in thumpy, undead pantomime. In time, Suneep and his gang would have a batch of telepresence robots up and running, and we'd move to them, get them wandering the queue area, interacting with curious guests. The new Mansion would be open for business in forty-eight hours, albeit in stripped-down fashion. The scaffolding made for a nice weenie, a visual draw that would pull the hordes that thronged Debra's Hall of Presidents over for a curious peek or two. Buzz city.

I'm a pretty smart guy.

• • •

Dan paged this Kim person and spoke to her as she was debarking the Pirates of the Caribbean. I wondered if she was the right person for the job: she seemed awfully enamored of the rehabs that Debra and her crew had performed. If I'd had more time, I would've run a deep background check on every one of the names on my list, but that would've taken months.

Dan made some small talk with Kim, speaking aloud in deference to my handicap, before coming to the point. "We read your post about the Mansion's rehab. You're the first one to notice it, and we wondered if you'd be interested in coming by to find out a little more about our plans."

Dan winced. "She's a screamer," he whispered.

Reflexively, I tried to pull up a HUD with my files on the Mansion fans we hoped to recruit. Of course, nothing happened. I'd done that a dozen times that morning, and there was no end in sight. I couldn't seem to get lathered up about it, though, nor about anything else, not even the hickey just visible under Dan's collar. The transdermal mood-balancer on my bicep was seeing to that—doctor's orders.

"Fine, fine. We're standing by the Pet Cemetery, two cast members, male, in Mansion costumes. About five-ten, apparent thirty. You can't miss us."

She didn't. She arrived out of breath and excited, jogging. She was apparent twenty, and dressed like a real twenty-year-old, in a hipster climate-control cowl that clung to and released her limbs, which were long and double-kneed. All the rage among the younger set, including the girl who'd shot me.

But the resemblance to my killer ended with her dress and body. She wasn't wearing a designer face, rather one that had enough imperfections to be the one she was born with, eyes set close and nose wide and slightly squashed.

I admired the way she moved through the crowd, fast and low but without jostling anyone. "Kim," I called as she drew near. "Over here."

She gave a happy shriek and made a beeline for us. Even charging full-bore, she was good enough at navigating the crowd that she didn't brush against a single soul. When she reached us, she came up short and bounced a little. "Hi, I'm Kim!" she said, pumping my arm with the peculiar violence of the extra-jointed. "Julius," I said, then waited while she repeated the process with Dan.

"So," she said, "what's the deal?"

I took her hand. "Kim, we've got a job for you, if you're interested."

She squeezed my hand hard and her eyes shone. "I'll take it!" she said.

I laughed, and so did Dan. It was a polite, castmembery sort of laugh, but underneath it was relief. "I think I'd better explain it to you first," I said.

"Explain away!" she said, and gave my hand another squeeze.

I let go of her hand and ran down an abbreviated

version of the rehab plans, leaving out anything about Debra and her ad-hocs. Kim drank it all in greedily. She cocked her head at me as I ran it down, eyes wide. It was disconcerting, and I finally asked, "Are you recording this?"

Kim blushed. "I hope that's OK! I'm starting a new Mansion scrapbook. I have one for every ride in the Park, but this one's gonna be a world-beater!"

Here was something I hadn't thought about. Publishing ad-hoc business was tabu inside Park, so much so that it hadn't occurred me that the new castmembers we brought in would want to record every little detail and push it out over the Net as a big old Whuffie collector.

"I can switch it off," Kim said. She looked worried, and I really started to grasp how important the Mansion was to the people we were recruiting, how much of a privilege we were offering them.

"Leave it rolling," I said. "Let's show the world how it's done."

We led Kim into a utilidor and down to costuming. She was half-naked by the time we got there, literally tearing off her clothes in anticipation of getting into character. Sonya, a Liberty Square ad-hoc that we'd stashed at costuming, already had clothes waiting for her, a rotting maid's uniform with an oversized toolbelt.

We left Kim on the scaffolding, energetically troweling a water-based cement substitute onto the wall, scraping it off and moving to a new spot. It looked boring to me, but I could believe that we'd have to tear her away when the time came.

We went back to trawling the Net for the next candidate.

By lunchtime, there were ten drilling, hammering, troweling new castmembers around the scaffolding, pushing black wheelbarrows, singing "Grim Grinning Ghosts" and generally having a high old time.

"This'll do," I said to Dan. I was exhausted and soaked with sweat, and the transdermal under my costume itched. Despite the happy-juice in my bloodstream, a streak of uncastmemberly crankiness was shot through my mood. I needed to get offstage.

Dan helped me hobble away, and as we hit the utilidor, he whispered in my ear, "This was a great idea, Julius. Really."

We jumped a tram over to Imagineering, my chest swollen with pride. Suneep had three of his assistants working on the first generation of mobile telepresence robots for the exterior, and had promised a prototype for that afternoon. The robots were easy enough—just off-the-shelf stuff, really—but the costumes and kinematics routines were something else. Thinking about what he and Suneep's gang of hypercreative supergeniuses would come up with cheered me up a little, as did being out of the public eye.

Suneep's lab looked like it had been hit by a tornado. Imagineer packs rolled in and out with arcane gizmos, or formed tight argumentative knots in the corners as they shouted over whatever their HUDs were displaying. In the middle of it all was Suneep, who looked like he was barely restraining an urge to shout Yippee! He was clearly in his element.

He threw his arms open when he caught sight of Dan and me, threw them wide enough to embrace the whole mad, gibbering chaos. "What wonderful flumgubbery!" he shouted over the noise.

"Sure is," I agreed. "How's the prototype coming?"

Suneep waved absently, his short fingers describing trivialities in the air. "In due time, in due time. I've put that team onto something else, a kinematics routine for a class of flying spooks that use gasbags to stay aloft—silent and scary. It's old spy-tech, and the retrofit's coming tremendously. Take a look!" He pointed a finger at me and, presumably, squirted some data my way.

"I'm offline," I reminded him gently.

He slapped his forehead, took a moment to push his hair off his face, and gave me an apologetic wave. "Of course, of course. Here." He unrolled an LCD and handed it to me. A flock of spooks danced on the screen, rendered against the ballroom scene. They were thematically consistent with the existing Mansion ghosts, more funny than scary, and their faces were familiar. I looked around the lab and realized that they'd caricatured various Imagineers.

"Ah! You noticed," Suneep said, rubbing his hands together. "A very good joke, yes?"

"This is terrific," I said, carefully. "But I really need some robots up and running by tomorrow night, Suneep. We discussed this, remember?" Without telepresence robots, my recruiting would be limited to fans like Kim, who lived in the area. I had broader designs than that.

Suneep looked disappointed. "Of course. We discussed it. I don't like to stop my people when they have good ideas, but there's a time and a place. I'll put them on it right away. Leave it to me."

Dan turned to greet someone, and I looked to see who it was. Lil. Of course. She was raccoon-eyed with fatigue, and she reached out for Dan's hand, saw me, and changed her mind.

"Hi, guys," she said, with studied casualness.

"Oh, hello!" said Suneep. He fired his finger at her—the flying ghosts, I imagined. Lil's eyes rolled up for a moment, then she nodded exhaustedly at him.

"Very good," she said. "I just heard from Lisa. She says the indoor crews are on-schedule. They've got most of the animatronics dismantled, and they're taking down the glass in the Ballroom now." The Ballroom ghost effects were accomplished by means of a giant pane of polished glass that laterally bisected the room. The Mansion had been built around it—it was too big to take out in one piece. "They say it'll be a couple days before they've got it cut up and ready to remove."

A pocket of uncomfortable silence descended on us, the roar of the Imagineers rushing in to fill it.

"You must be exhausted," Dan said, at length.

"Goddamn right," I said, at the same moment that Lil said, "I guess I am."

We both smiled wanly. Suneep put his arms around Lil's and my shoulders and squeezed. He smelled of an exotic cocktail of industrial lubricant, ozone, and fatigue poisons.

"You two should go home and give each other a massage," he said. "You've earned some rest."

Dan met my eye and shook his head apologetically. I squirmed out from under Suneep's arm and thanked him quietly, then slunk off to the Contemporary for a hot tub and a couple hours of sleep.

I came back to the Mansion at sundown. It was cool enough that I took a surface route, costume rolled in a shoulderbag, instead of riding through the clattering, air-conditioned comfort of the utilidors.

As a freshening breeze blew across me, I suddenly had a craving for *real* weather, the kind of climate I'd grown up with in Toronto. It was October, for chrissakes, and a lifetime of conditioning told me that it was May. I stopped and leaned on a bench for a moment and closed my eyes. Unbidden, and with the clarity of a HUD, I saw High Park in Toronto, clothed in its autumn colors, fiery reds and oranges, shades of evergreen and earthy brown. God, I needed a vacation.

I opened my eyes and realized that I was standing

in front of the Hall of Presidents, and that there was a queue ahead of me for it, one that stretched back and back. I did a quick sum in my head and sucked air between my teeth: they had enough people for five or six full houses waiting here—easily an hour's wait. The Hall *never* drew crowds like this. Debra was working the turnstiles in Betsy Ross gingham, and she caught my eye and snapped a nod at me.

I stalked off to the Mansion. A choir of zombie-shambling new recruits had formed up in front of the gate, and were groaning their way through "Grim Grinning Ghosts," with a new call-and-response structure. A small audience participated, urged on by the recruits on the scaffolding.

"Well, at least that's going right," I muttered to myself. And it was, except that I could see members of the ad-hoc looking on from the sidelines, and the looks weren't kindly. Totally obsessive fans are a good measure of a ride's popularity, but they're kind of a pain in the ass, too. They lipsynch the soundtrack, cadge souvenirs and pester you with smarmy, show-off questions. After a while, even the cheeriest cast-member starts to lose patience, develop an automatic distaste for them.

The Liberty Square ad-hocs who were working on the Mansion had been railroaded into approving a rehab, press-ganged into working on it, and were now forced to endure the company of these grandstanding megafans. If I'd been there when it all started—instead of sleeping!—I may've been able to massage their bruised egos, but now I wondered if it was too late.

Nothing for it but to do it. I ducked into a utilidor, changed into my costume and went back onstage. I joined the call-and-response enthusiastically, walking around to the ad-hocs and getting them to join in, reluctantly or otherwise.

By the time the choir retired, sweaty and exhausted, a group of ad-hocs were ready to take their place, and I escorted my recruits to an offstage break-room.

Suneep didn't deliver the robot prototypes for a week, and told me that it would be another week before I could have even five production units. Though he didn't say it, I got the sense that his guys were out of control, so excited by the freedom from ad-hoc oversight that they were running wild. Suneep himself was nearly a wreck, nervous and jumpy. I didn't press it.

Besides, I had problems of my own. The new recruits were multiplying. I was staying on top of the fan response to the rehab from a terminal I'd had installed in my hotel room. Kim and her local colleagues were fielding millions of hits every day, their Whuffie accumulating as envious fans around the world logged in to watch their progress on the scaffolding.

That was all according to plan. What wasn't according to plan was that the new recruits were doing their own recruiting, extending invitations to their net-pals to come on down to Florida, bunk on their sofas and guest-beds, and present themselves to me for active duty.

The tenth time it happened, I approached Kim in the break room. Her gorge was working, her eyes tracked invisible words across the middle distance. No doubt she was penning yet another breathless missive about the magic of working in the Mansion. "Hey, there," I said. "Have you got a minute to meet with me?"

She held up a single finger, then, a moment later, gave me a bright smile.

"Hi, Julius!" she said. "Sure!"

"Why don't you change into civvies, we'll take a walk through the Park and talk?"

Kim wore her costume every chance she got. I'd been quite firm about her turning it in to the laundry every night instead of wearing it home.

Reluctantly, she stepped into a change-room and switched into her cowl. We took the utilidor to the Fantasyland exit and walked through the late-afternoon rush of children and their adults, queued deep and thick for Snow White, Dumbo and Peter Pan.

"How're you liking it here?" I asked.

Kim gave a little bounce. "Oh, Julius, it's the best time of my life, really! A dream come true. I'm meeting so many interesting people, and I'm really feeling creative. I can't wait to try out the telepresence rigs, too."

"Well, I'm really pleased with what you and your friends are up to here. You're working hard, putting on a good show. I like the songs you've been working up, too."

She did one of those double-kneed shuffles that was the basis of any number of action vids those days, and she was suddenly standing in front of me, hand on my shoulder, looking into my eyes. She looked serious.

"Is there a problem, Julius? If there is, I'd rather we just talked about it, instead of making chitchat."

I smiled and took her hand off my shoulder. "How old are you, Kim?"

"Nineteen," she said. "What's the problem?"

Nineteen! Jesus, no wonder she was so volatile. *What's my excuse, then?*

"It's not a problem, Kim, it's just something I wanted to discuss with you. The people you-all have been bringing down to work for me, they're all really great castmembers."

"But?"

"But we have limited resources around here. Not enough hours in the day for me to stay on top of the new folks, the rehab, everything. Not to mention that until we open the new Mansion, there's a limited number of extras we can use out front. I'm concerned that we're going to put someone on stage without proper training, or that we're going to run out of uniforms;

I'm also concerned about people coming all the way here and discovering that there aren't any shifts for them to take."

She gave me a relieved look. "Is *that* all? Don't worry about it. I've been talking to Debra, over at the Hall of Presidents, and she says she can pick up any people who can't be used at the Mansion—we could even rotate back and forth!" She was clearly proud of her foresight.

My ears buzzed. Debra, one step ahead of me all along the way. She probably suggested that Kim do some extra recruiting in the first place. She'd take in the people who came down to work the Mansion, convince them they'd been hard done by the Liberty Square crew, and rope them into her little Whuffie ranch, the better to seize the Mansion, the Park, the whole of Walt Disney World.

"Oh, I don't think it'll come to that," I said, carefully. "I'm sure we can find a use for them all at the Mansion. More the merrier."

Kim cocked quizzical, but let it go. I bit my tongue. The pain brought me back to reality, and I started planning costume production, training rosters, bunking. God, if only Suneep would finish the robots!

"What do you mean, 'no'?" I said, hotly.

Lil folded her arms and glared. "No, Julius. It won't fly. The group is already upset that all the glory is going to the new people, they'll never let us bring more in. They also won't stop working on the rehab to train them, costume them, feed them and mother them. They're losing Whuffie every day that the Mansion's shut up, and they don't want any more delays. Dave's already joined up with Debra, and I'm sure he's not the last one."

Dave—the jerk who'd pissed all over the rehab in the meeting. Of course he'd gone over. Lil and Dan stood side by side on the porch of the house where I'd lived. I'd driven out that night to convince Lil to sell the ad-hocs on bringing in more recruits, but it wasn't going according to plan. They wouldn't even let me in the house.

"So what do I tell Kim?"

"Tell her whatever you want," Lil said. "You brought her in—you manage her. Take some goddamn responsibility for once in your life."

It wasn't going to get any better. Dan gave me an apologetic look. Lil glared a moment longer, then went into the house.

"Debra's doing real well," he said. "The net's all over her. Biggest thing ever. Flash-baking is taking off in nightclubs, dance mixes with the DJ's backup being shoved in bursts into the dancers."

"God," I said. "I fucked up, Dan. I fucked it all up."

He didn't say anything, and that was the same as agreeing.

Driving back to the hotel, I decided I needed to talk to Kim. She was a problem I didn't need, and maybe a problem I could solve. I pulled a screeching U-turn and drove the little runabout to her place, a tiny condo in a crumbling complex that had once been a gated seniors' village, pre-Bitchun.

Her place was easy to spot. All the lights were burning, faint conversation audible through the screen door. I jogged up the steps two at a time, and was about to knock when a familiar voice drifted through the screen.

Debra, saying: "Oh yes, oh yes! Terrific idea! I'd never really thought about using streetmosphere players to liven up the queue area, but you're making a lot of sense. You people have just been doing the *best* work over at the Mansion—find me more like you and I'll take them for the Hall any day!"

I heard Kim and her young friends chatting excitedly, proudly. The anger and fear suffused me from tip to toe, and I felt suddenly light and cool and ready to do something terrible.

I padded silently down the steps and got into my runabout.

Some people never learn. I'm one of them, apparently.

I almost chortled over the foolproof simplicity of my plan as I slipped in through the cast entrance using the ID card I'd scored when my systems went offline and I was no longer able to squirt my authorization at the door.

I changed clothes in a bathroom on Main Street,

switching into a black cowl that completely obscured my features, then slunk through the shadows along the storefronts until I came to the moat around Cinderella's castle. Keeping low, I stepped over the fence and duck-walked down the embankment, then slipped into the water and sloshed across to the Adventureland side.

Slipping along to the Liberty Square gateway, I flattened myself in doorways whenever I heard maintenance crews passing in the distance, until I reached the Hall of Presidents, and in a twinkling I was inside the theater itself.

Humming the Small World theme, I produced a short wrecking bar from my cowl's tabbed pocket and set to work.

The primary broadcast units were hidden behind a painted scrim over the stage, and they were surprisingly well built for a first generation tech. I really worked up a sweat smashing them, but I kept at it until not a single component remained recognizable. The work was slow and loud in the silent Park, but it lulled me into a sleepy reverie, an autohypnotic swing-bang-swing-bang timeless time. To be on the safe side, I grabbed the storage units and slipped them into the cowl.

Locating their backup units was a little trickier, but years of hanging out at the Hall of Presidents while Lil tinkered with the animatronics helped me. I methodically investigated every nook, cranny and storage area until I located them, in what had been a break room closet. By now, I had the rhythm of the thing, and I made short work of them.

I did one more pass, wrecking anything that looked like it might be a prototype for the next generation or notes that would help them reconstruct the units I'd smashed.

I had no illusions about Debra's preparedness—she'd have something offsite that she could get up and running in a few days. I wasn't doing anything permanent, I was just buying myself a day or two.

I made my way clean out of the Park without being spotted, and sloshed my way into my runabout, shoes leaking water from the moat.

For the first time in weeks, I slept like a baby.

Of course, I got caught. I don't really have the temperament for Machiavellian shenanigans, and I left a trail a mile wide, from the muddy footprints in the Contemporary's lobby to the wrecking bar thoughtlessly left behind, with my cowl and the storage units from the Hall, forgotten on the back seat of my runabout.

I whistled my personal jazzy uptempo version of "Grim Grinning Ghosts" as I made my way from Costuming, through the utilidor, out to Liberty Square, half an hour before the Park opened.

Standing in front of me were Lil and Debra. Debra was holding my cowl and wrecking bar. Lil held the storage units.

I hadn't put on my transdermals that morning, and so the emotion I felt was unmuffled, loud and yammering.

I ran.

I ran past them, along the road to Adventureland, past the Tiki Room where I'd been killed, past the Adventureland gate where I'd waded through the moat, down Main Street. I ran and ran, elbowing early guests, trampling flowers, knocking over an apple cart across from the Penny Arcade.

I ran until I reached the main gate, and turned, thinking I'd outrun Lil and Debra and all my problems. I'd thought wrong. They were both there, a step behind me, puffing and red. Debra held my wrecking bar like a weapon, and she brandished it at me.

"You're a goddamn idiot, you know that?" she said. I think if we'd been alone, she would've swung it at me.

"Can't take it when someone else plays rough, huh, Debra?" I sneered.

Lil shook her head disgustedly. "She's right, you are an idiot. The ad-hoc's meeting in Adventureland. You're coming."

"Why?" I asked, feeling belligerent. "You going to honor me for all my hard work?"

"We're going to talk about the future, Julius, what's left of it for us."

"For God's sake, Lil, can't you see what's going on? They *killed* me! They did it, and now we're fighting each other instead of her! Why can't you see how *wrong* that is?"

"You'd better watch those accusations, Julius," Debra said, quietly and intensely, almost hissing. "I don't know who killed you or why, but you're the one who's guilty here. You need help."

I barked a humorless laugh. Guests were starting to stream into the now-open Park, and several of them were watching intently as the three costumed castmembers shouted at each other. I could feel my Whuffie hemorrhaging. "Debra, you are purely full of shit, and your work is trite and unimaginative. You're a fucking despoiler and you don't even have the guts to admit it."

"That's *enough,* Julius," Lil said, her face hard, her rage barely in check. "We're going."

Debra walked a pace behind me, Lil a pace before, all the way through the crowd to Adventureland. I saw a dozen opportunities to slip into a gap in the human ebb and flow and escape custody, but I didn't try. I wanted a chance to tell the whole world what I'd done and why I'd done it.

Debra followed us in when we mounted the steps to the meeting room. Lil turned. "I don't think you should be here, Debra," she said in measured tones.

Debra shook her head. "You can't keep me out, you know. And you shouldn't want to. We're on the same side."

I snorted derisively, and I think it decided Lil. "Come on, then," she said.

It was SRO in the meeting room, packed to the gills with the entire ad-hoc, except for my new recruits. No work was being done on the rehab, then, and the Liberty Belle would be sitting at her dock. Even the restaurant crews were there. Liberty Square must've been a ghost town. It gave the meeting a sense of urgency: the knowledge that there were guests in Liberty Square wandering aimlessly, looking for castmembers to help them out. Of course, Debra's crew might've been around.

The crowd's faces were hard and bitter, leaving no doubt in my mind that I was in deep shit. Even Dan, sitting in the front row, looked angry. I nearly started crying right then. Dan—oh, Dan. My pal, my confidant, my patsy, my rival, my nemesis. Dan, Dan, Dan. I wanted to beat him to death and hug him at the same time.

Lil took the podium and tucked stray hairs behind her ears. "All right, then," she said. I stood to her left and Debra stood to her right.

"Thanks for coming out today. I'd like to get this done quickly. We all have important work to get to. I'll run down the facts: last night, a member of this ad-hoc vandalized the Hall of Presidents, rendering it useless. It's estimated that it will take at least a week to get it back up and running.

"I don't have to tell you that this isn't acceptable. This has never happened before, and it will never happen again. We're going to see to that.

"I'd like to propose that no further work be done on

the Mansion until the Hall of Presidents is fully operational. I will be volunteering my services on the repairs."

There were nods in the audience. Lil wouldn't be the only one working at the Hall that week. "Disney World isn't a competition," Lil said. "All the different ad-hocs work together, and we do it to make the Park as good as we can. We lose sight of that at our peril."

I nearly gagged on bile. "I'd like to say something," I said, as calmly as I could manage.

Lil shot me a look. "That's fine, Julius. Any member of the ad-hoc can speak."

I took a deep breath. "I did it, all right?" I said. My voice cracked. "I did it, and I don't have any excuse for having done it. It may not have been the smartest thing I've ever done, but I think you all should understand how I was driven to it.

"We're not *supposed* to be in competition with one another here, but we all know that that's just a polite fiction. The truth is that there's real competition in the Park, and that the hardest players are the crew that rehabbed the Hall of Presidents. They *stole* the Hall from you! They did it while you were distracted, they used *me* to engineer the distraction, they *murdered* me!" I heard the shriek creeping into my voice, but I couldn't do anything about it.

"Usually, the lie that we're all on the same side is fine. It lets us work together in peace. But that changed the day they had me shot. If you keep on believing it, you're going to lose the Mansion, the Liberty Belle, Tom Sawyer Island—all of it. All the history we have with this place—all the history that the billions who've visited it have—it's going to be destroyed and replaced with the sterile, thoughtless shit that's taken over the Hall. Once that happens, there's nothing left that makes this place special. Anyone can get the same experience sitting at home on the sofa! What happens then, huh? How much longer do you think this place will stay open once the only people here are *you?*"

Debra smiled condescendingly. "Are you finished, then?" she asked, sweetly. "Fine. I know I'm not a member of this group, but since it was my work that was destroyed last night, I think I would like to address Julius's statements, if you don't mind." She paused, but no one spoke up.

"First of all, I want you all to know that we don't hold you responsible for what happened last night. We know who was responsible, and he needs help. I urge you to see to it that he gets it.

"Next, I'd like to say that as far as I'm concerned, we are on the same side—the side of the Park. This is a special place, and it couldn't exist without all of our contributions. What happened to Julius was terrible, and I sincerely hope that the person responsible is caught and brought to justice. But that person wasn't me or any of the people in my ad-hoc.

"Lil, I'd like to thank you for your generous offer of assistance, and we'll take you up on it. That goes for all of you—come on by the Hall, we'll put you to work. We'll be up and running in no time.

"Now, as far as the Mansion goes, let me say this once and for all: neither me nor my ad-hoc have any desire to take over the operations of the Mansion. It is a terrific attraction, and it's getting better with the work you're all doing. If you've been worrying about it, then you can stop worrying now. We're all on the same side.

"Thanks for hearing me out. I've got to go see my team now."

She turned and left, a chorus of applause following her out.

Lil waited until it died down, then said, "All right, then, we've got work to do, too. I'd like to ask you all a favor, first. I'd like us to keep the details of last night's incident to ourselves. Letting the guests and the world know about this ugly business isn't good for anyone. Can we all agree to do that?"

There was a moment's pause while the results were tabulated on the HUDs, then Lil gave them a million-dollar smile. "I knew you'd come through. Thanks, guys. Let's get to work."

I spent the day at the hotel, listlessly scrolling around on my terminal. Lil had made it very clear to me after the meeting that I wasn't to show my face inside the Park until I'd "gotten help," whatever that meant.

By noon, the news was out. It was hard to pin down the exact source, but it seemed to revolve around the new recruits. One of them had told their net-pals about the high drama in Liberty Square, and mentioned my name.

There were already a couple of sites vilifying me, and I expected more. I needed some kind of help, that was for sure.

I thought about leaving then, turning my back on the whole business and leaving Walt Disney World to start yet another new life, Whuffie-poor and fancy-free.

It wouldn't be so bad. I'd been in poor repute before, not so long ago. That first time Dan and I had palled around, back at the U of T, I'd been the center of a lot of pretty ambivalent sentiment, and Whuffie-poor as a man can be.

I slept in a little coffin on-campus, perfectly climate-controlled. It was cramped and dull, but my access to the network was free and I had plenty of material to entertain myself. While I couldn't get a table in a restaurant, I was free to queue up at any of the makers around town and get myself whatever I wanted to eat and drink, whenever I wanted it. Compared to 99.99999 percent of all the people who'd ever lived, I had a life of unparalleled luxury.

Even by the standards of the Bitchun Society, I was hardly a rarity. The number of low-esteem individuals at large was significant, and they got along just fine, hanging out in parks, arguing, reading, staging plays, playing music.

Of course, that wasn't the life for me. I had Dan to pal around with, a rare high-net-Whuffie individual who was willing to fraternize with a shmuck like me. He'd stand me to meals at sidewalk cafes and concerts at the SkyDome, and shoot down any snotty reputation-punk who sneered at my Whuffie tally. Being with Dan was a process of constantly reevaluating my beliefs in the Bitchun Society, and I'd never had a more vibrant, thought-provoking time in all my life.

I could have left the Park, deadheaded to anywhere in the world, started over. I could have turned my back on Dan, on Debra, on Lil and the whole mess.

I didn't.

I called up the doc.

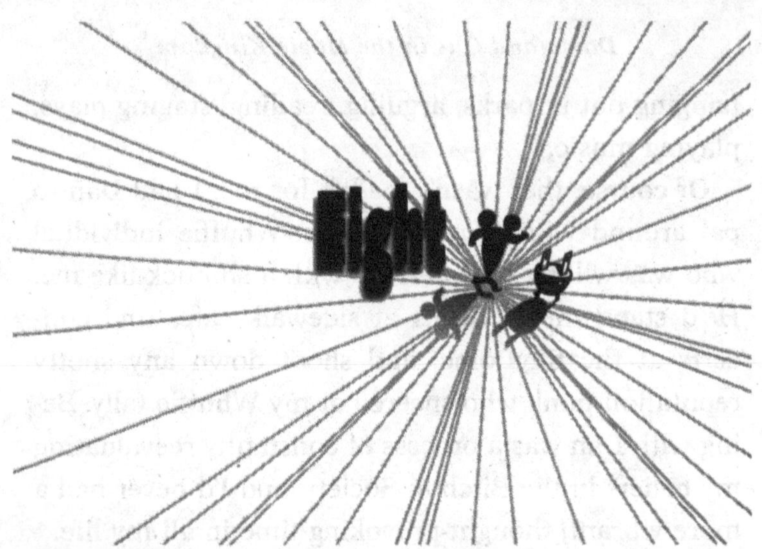

Doctor Pete answered on the third ring, audio-only. In the background, I heard a chorus of crying children, the constant backdrop of the Magic Kingdom infirmary.

"Hi, doc," I said.

"Hello, Julius. What can I do for you?" Under the veneer of professional medical and castmember friendliness, I sensed irritation.

Make it all good again. "I'm not really sure. I wanted to see if I could talk it over with you. I'm having some pretty big problems."

"I'm on-shift until five. Can it wait until then?"

By then, I had no idea if I'd have the nerve to see him. "I don't think so—I was hoping we could meet right away."

"If it's an emergency, I can have an ambulance sent for you."

"It's urgent, but not an emergency. I need to talk about it in person. Please?"

He sighed in undoctorly, uncastmemberly fashion. "Julius, I've got important things to do here. Are you sure this can't wait?"

I bit back a sob. "I'm sure, doc."

"All right then. When can you be here?"

Lil had made it clear that she didn't want me in the Park. "Can you meet me? I can't really come to you. I'm at the Contemporary, Tower B, room 2334."

"I don't really make house calls, son."

"I know, I know." I hated how pathetic I sounded. "Can you make an exception? I don't know who else to turn to."

"I'll be there as soon as I can. I'll have to get someone to cover for me. Let's not make a habit of this, all right?"

I whooshed out my relief. "I promise."

He disconnected abruptly, and I found myself dialing Dan.

"Yes?" he said, cautiously.

"Doctor Pete is coming over, Dan. I don't know if he can help me—I don't know if anyone can. I just wanted you to know."

He surprised me, then, and made me remember why he was still my friend, even after everything. "Do you want me to come over?"

"That would be very nice," I said, quietly. "I'm at the hotel."

"Give me ten minutes," he said, and rang off.

• • •

He found me on my patio, looking out at the Castle and the peaks of Space Mountain. To my left spread the sparkling waters of the Seven Seas Lagoon, to my right, the Property stretched away for mile after manicured mile. The sun was warm on my skin, faint strains of happy laughter drifted with the wind, and the flowers were in bloom. In Toronto, it would be freezing rain, gray buildings, noisy rapid transit (a monorail hissed by), and hard-faced anonymity. I missed it.

Dan pulled up a chair next to mine and sat without a word. We both stared out at the view for a long while.

"It's something else, isn't it?" I said, finally.

"I suppose so," he said. "I want to say something before the doc comes by, Julius."

"Go ahead."

"Lil and I are through. It should never have happened in the first place, and I'm not proud of myself. If you two were breaking up, that's none of my business, but I had no right to hurry it along."

"All right," I said. I was too drained for emotion.

"I've taken a room here, moved my things."

"How's Lil taking it?"

"Oh, she thinks I'm a total bastard. I suppose she's right."

"I suppose she's partly right," I corrected him.

He gave me a gentle slug in the shoulder. "Thanks."

We waited in companionable silence until the doc arrived.

He bustled in, his smile lines drawn up into a sour purse, and waited expectantly. I left Dan on the patio while I took a seat on the bed.

"I'm cracking up or something," I said. "I've been acting erratically, sometimes violently. I don't know what's wrong with me." I'd rehearsed the speech, but it still wasn't easy to choke out.

"We both know what's wrong, Julius," the doc said, impatiently. "You need to be refreshed from your backup, get set up with a fresh clone and retire this one. We've had this talk."

"I can't do it," I said, not meeting his eye. "I just can't—isn't there another way?"

The doc shook his head. "Julius, I've got limited resources to allocate. There's a perfectly good cure for what's ailing you, and if you won't take it, there's not much I can do for you."

"But what about meds?"

"Your problem isn't a chemical imbalance, it's a mental defect. Your *brain* is *broken*, son. All that meds will do is mask the symptoms while you get worse. I can't tell you what you want to hear, unfortunately. Now, If you're ready to take the cure, I can retire this clone immediately and get you restored into a new one in forty-eight hours."

"Isn't there another way? Please? You have to help me—I can't lose all this." I couldn't admit my real reasons for being so attached to this singularly miserable chapter in my life, not even to myself.

The doctor rose to go. "Look, Julius, you haven't got

the Whuffie to make it worth anyone's time to research a solution to this problem, other than the one that we all know about. I can give you mood-suppressants, but that's not a permanent solution."

"Why not?"

He boggled. "You *can't* just take dope for the rest of your life, son. Eventually, something will happen to this body—I see from your file that you're stroke-prone—and you're going to get refreshed from your backup. The longer you wait, the more traumatic it'll be. You're robbing from your future self for your selfish present."

It wasn't the first time the thought had crossed my mind. Every passing day made it harder to take the cure. To lie down and wake up friends with Dan, to wake up and be in love with Lil again. To wake up to a Mansion the way I remembered it, a Hall of Presidents where I could find Lil bent over with her head in a President's guts of an afternoon. To lie down and wake without disgrace, without knowing that my lover and my best friend would betray me, *had* betrayed me.

I just couldn't do it—not yet, anyway.

Dan—Dan was going to kill himself soon, and if I restored myself from my old backup, I'd lose my last year with him. I'd lose *his* last year.

"Let's table that, doc. I hear what you're saying, but there're complications. I guess I'll take the mood-suppressants for now."

He gave me a cold look. "I'll give you a scrip, then.

I could've done that without coming out here. Please don't call me anymore."

I was shocked by his obvious ire, but I didn't understand it until he was gone and I told Dan what had happened.

"Us old-timers, we're used to thinking of doctors as highly trained professionals—all that pre-Bitchun med-school stuff, long internships, anatomy drills . . . Truth is, the average doc today gets more training in bedside manner than bioscience. 'Doctor' Pete is a technician, not an MD, not the way you and I mean it. Anyone with the kind of knowledge you're looking for is working as a historical researcher, not a doctor.

"But that's not the illusion. The doc is supposed to be the authority on medical matters, even though he's only got one trick: restore from backup. You're reminding Pete of that, and he's not happy to have it happen."

I waited a week before returning to the Magic Kingdom, sunning myself on the white sand beach at the Contemporary, jogging the Walk Around the World, taking a canoe out to the wild and overgrown Discovery Island, and generally cooling out. Dan came by in the evenings and it was like old times, running down the pros and cons of Whuffie and Bitchunry and life in general, sitting on my porch with a sweating pitcher of lemonade.

On the last night, he presented me with a clever little handheld, a museum piece that I recalled fondly from the dawning days of the Bitchun Society. It had much of the functionality of my defunct systems, in a package I could slip in my shirt pocket. It felt like part of a costume, like the turnip watches the Ben Franklin streetmosphere players wore at the American Adventure.

Museum piece or no, it meant that I was once again qualified to participate in the Bitchun Society, albeit more slowly and less efficiently than I once may've. I took it downstairs the next morning and drove to the Magic Kingdom's castmember lot.

At least, that was the plan. When I got down to the Contemporary's parking lot, my runabout was gone. A quick check with the handheld revealed the worst: my Whuffie was low enough that someone had just gotten inside and driven away, realizing that they could make more popular use of it than I could.

With a sinking feeling, I trudged up to my room and swiped my key through the lock. It emitted a soft, unsatisfied *bzzz* and lit up, "Please see the front desk." My room had been reassigned, too. I had the short end of the Whuffie stick.

At least there was no mandatory Whuffie check on the monorail platform, but the other people on the car were none too friendly to me, and no one offered me an inch more personal space than was necessary. I had hit bottom.

• • •

I took the castmember entrance to the Magic Kingdom, clipping my name tag to my Disney Operations polo shirt, ignoring the glares of my fellow castmembers in the utilidors.

I used the handheld to page Dan. "Hey there," he said, brightly. I could tell instantly that I was being humored.

"Where are you?" I asked.

"Oh, up in the Square. By the Liberty Tree."

In front of the Hall of Presidents. I worked the handheld, pinged some Whuffie manually. Debra was spiked so high it seemed she'd never come down, as were Tim and her whole crew in aggregate. They were drawing from guests by the millions, and from castmembers and from people who'd read the popular accounts of their struggle against the forces of petty jealousy and sabotage—i.e., me.

I felt light-headed. I hurried along to costuming and changed into the heavy green Mansion costume, then ran up the stairs to the Square.

I found Dan sipping a coffee and sitting on a bench under the giant, lantern-hung Liberty Tree. He had a second cup waiting for me, and patted the bench next to him. I sat with him and sipped, waiting for him to spill whatever bit of rotten news he had for me this morning—I could feel it hovering like storm clouds.

He wouldn't talk though, not until we finished the coffee. Then he stood and strolled over to the Mansion. It wasn't rope-drop yet, and there weren't any guests in the Park, which was all for the better, given what was coming next.

"Have you taken a look at Debra's Whuffie lately?" he asked, finally, as we stood by the pet cemetery, considering the empty scaffolding.

I started to pull out the handheld but he put a hand on my arm. "Don't bother," he said, morosely. "Suffice it to say, Debra's gang is number one with a bullet. Ever since word got out about what happened to the Hall, they've been stacking it deep. They can do just about anything, Jules, and get away with it."

My stomach tightened and I found myself grinding my molars. "So, what is it they've done, Dan?" I asked, already knowing the answer.

Dan didn't have to respond, because at that moment, Tim emerged from the Mansion, wearing a light cotton work-smock. He had a thoughtful expression, and when he saw us, he beamed his elfin grin and came over.

"Hey guys!" he said.

"Hi, Tim," Dan said. I nodded, not trusting myself to speak.

"Pretty exciting stuff, huh?" he said.

"I haven't told him yet," Dan said, with forced lightness. "Why don't you run it down?"

"Well, it's pretty radical, I have to admit. We've learned some stuff from the Hall that we wanted to apply, and at the same time, we wanted to capture some of the historical character of the ghost story."

I opened my mouth to object, but Dan put a hand on my forearm. "Really?" he asked innocently. "How do you plan on doing that?"

"Well, we're keeping the telepresence robots—that's a honey of an idea, Julius—but we're giving each one an uplink so that it can flash-bake. We've got some high-Whuffie horror writers pulling together a series of narratives about the lives of each ghost: how they met their tragic ends, what they've done since, you know.

"The way we've storyboarded it, the guests stream through the ride pretty much the way they do now, walking through the preshow and then getting into the ride-vehicles, the Doom Buggies. But here's the big change: we *slow it all down.* We trade off throughput for intensity, make it more of a premium product.

"So you're a guest. From the queue to the unload zone, you're being chased by these ghosts, these telepresence robots, and they're really scary—I've got Suneep's concept artists going back to the drawing board, hitting basic research on stuff that'll just scare the guests silly. When a ghost catches you, lays its hands on you—wham! Flash-bake! You get its whole grisly story in three seconds, across your frontal lobe. By the time you've left, you've had ten or more ghost-contacts, and the next time you come back, it's all new ghosts with all new stories. The way that the Hall's drawing 'em, we're bound to be a hit." He put his hands behind his back and rocked on his heels, clearly proud of himself.

When Epcot Center first opened, long, long ago, there'd been an ugly decade or so in ride design. Imagineering found a winning formula for Spaceship Earth, the flagship ride in the big golf ball, and, in their drive to establish thematic continuity, they'd turned the formula into a cookie-cutter, stamping out half a dozen clones for each of the "themed" areas in the Future Showcase. It went like this: first, we were cavemen, then there was ancient Greece, then Rome burned (cue sulfur-odor FX), then there was the Great Depression, and, finally, we reached the modern age. Who knows what the future holds? We do! We'll all have videophones and be living on the ocean floor. Once was cute—compelling and inspirational, even—but six times was embarrassing. Like everyone, once Imagineering got themselves a good hammer, everything started to resemble a nail. Even now, the Epcot ad-hocs were repeating the sins of their forebears, closing every ride with a scene of Bitchun utopia.

And Debra was repeating the classic mistake, tearing her way through the Magic Kingdom with her blaster set to flash-bake.

"Tim," I said, hearing the tremble in my voice. "I thought you said that you had no designs on the Mansion, that you and Debra wouldn't be trying to take it away from us. Didn't you say that?"

Tim rocked back as if I'd slapped him and the blood drained from his face. "But we're not taking it away!" he said. "You *invited* us to help."

I shook my head, confused. "We did?" I said.

"Sure," he said.

"Yes," Dan said. "Kim and some of the other rehab cast went to Debra yesterday and asked her to do a design review of the current rehab and suggest any changes. She was good enough to agree, and they've come up with some great ideas." I read between the lines: the newbies you invited in have gone over to the other side and we're going to lose everything because of them. I felt like shit.

"Well, I stand corrected," I said, carefully. Tim's grin came back and he clapped his hands together. *He really loves the Mansion,* I thought. *He could have been on our side, if we had only played it all right.*

Dan and I took to the utilidors and grabbed a pair of bicycles and sped towards Suneep's lab, jangling our bells at the rushing castmembers. "They don't have the authority to invite Debra in," I panted as we pedaled.

"Says who?" Dan said.

"It was part of the deal—they knew that they were probationary members right from the start. They weren't even allowed into the design meetings."

"Looks like they took themselves off probation," he said.

Suneep gave us both a chilly look when we entered his lab. He had dark circles under his eyes and his hands shook with exhaustion. He seemed to be holding himself erect with nothing more than raw anger.

"So much for building without interference," he

said. "We agreed that this project wouldn't change midway through. Now it has, and I've got other commitments that I'm going to have to cancel because this is going off-schedule."

I made soothing apologetic gestures with my hands. "Suneep, believe me, I'm just as upset about this as you are. We don't like this one little bit."

He harrumphed. "We had a deal, Julius," he said, hotly. "I would do the rehab for you and you would keep the ad-hocs off my back. I've been holding up my end of the bargain, but where the hell have you been? If they replan the rehab now, I'll *have* to go along with them. I can't just leave the Mansion half-done—they'll murder me."

The kernel of a plan formed in my mind. "Suneep, we don't like the new rehab plan, and we're going to stop it. You can help. Just stonewall them—tell them they'll have to find other Imagineering support if they want to go through with it, that you're booked solid."

Dan gave me one of his long, considering looks, then nodded a minute approval. "Yeah," he drawled. "That'll help all right. Just tell 'em that they're welcome to make any changes they want to the plan, *if* they can find someone else to execute them."

Suneep looked unhappy. "Fine—so then they go and find someone else to do it, and that person gets all the credit for the work my team's done so far. I just flush my time down the toilet."

"It won't come to that," I said quickly. "If you can

just keep saying no for a couple days, we'll do the rest."

Suneep looked doubtful.

"I promise," I said.

Suneep ran his stubby fingers through his already crazed hair. "All right," he said, morosely.

Dan slapped him on the back. "Good man," he said.

It should have worked. It almost did.

I sat in the back of the Adventureland conference room while Dan exhorted.

"Look, you don't have to roll over for Debra and her people! This is *your* garden, and you've tended it responsibly for years. She's got no right to move in on you—you've got all the Whuffie you need to defend the place, if you all work together."

No castmember likes confrontation, and the Liberty Square bunch were tough to rouse to action. Dan had turned down the air conditioning an hour before the meeting and closed up all the windows, so that the room was a kiln for hard-firing irritation into rage. I stood meekly in the back, as far as possible from Dan. He was working his magic on my behalf, and I was content to let him do his thing.

When Lil had arrived, she'd sized up the situation with a sour expression: sit in the front, near Dan, or in the back, near me. She'd chosen the middle, and to concentrate on Dan I had to tear my eyes away from the sweat glistening on her long, pale neck.

Dan stalked the aisles like a preacher, eyes blazing. "They're *stealing* your future! They're *stealing* your *past!* They claim they've got your support!"

He lowered his tone. "I don't think that's true." He grabbed a castmember by her hand and looked into her eyes. "Is it true?" he said so low it was almost a whisper.

"No," the castmember said.

He dropped her hand and whirled to face another castmember. "Is it true?" he demanded, raising his voice, slightly.

"No!" the castmember said, his voice unnaturally loud after the whispers. A nervous chuckle rippled through the crowd.

"Is it true?" he said, striding to the podium, shouting now.

"No!" the crowd roared.

"NO!" he shouted back.

"You don't *have to* roll over and take it! You can fight back, carry on with the plan, send them packing. They're only taking over because you're letting them. Are you going to let them?"

"NO!"

Bitchun wars are rare. Long before anyone tries a takeover of anything, they've done the arithmetic and ensured themselves that the ad-hoc they're displacing doesn't have a hope of fighting back.

For the defenders, it's a simple decision: step down gracefully and salvage some reputation out of the thing—fighting back will surely burn away even that meager reward.

No one benefits from fighting back—least of all the thing everyone's fighting over. For example:

It was the second year of my undergrad, taking a double-major in not making trouble for my profs and keeping my mouth shut. It was the early days of Bitchun, and most of us were still a little unclear on the concept.

Not all of us, though: a group of campus shit-disturbers, grad students in the Sociology Department, were on the bleeding edge of the revolution, and they knew what they wanted: control of the Department, oustering of the tyrannical, stodgy profs, a bully pulpit from which to preach the Bitchun gospel to a generation of impressionable undergrads who were too cowed by their workloads to realize what a load of shit they were being fed by the University.

At least, that's what the intense, heavyset woman who seized the mic at my Soc 200 course said, that sleepy morning mid-semester at Convocation Hall. Nineteen hundred students filled the hall, a capacity crowd of bleary, coffee-sipping time-markers, and they woke up in a hurry when the woman's strident harangue burst over their heads.

I saw it happen from the very start. The prof was down there on the stage, a speck with a tie-mic, droning over his slides, and then there was a blur as half a dozen grad students rushed the stage. They were dressed in University poverty-chic, wrinkled slacks and tattered sports coats, and five of them formed a human wall in front of the prof while the sixth, the heavyset one with the dark hair and the prominent mole on her cheek, unclipped his mic and clipped it to her lapel.

"Wakey wakey!" she called, and the reality of the moment hit home for me: this wasn't on the lesson-plan.

"Come on, heads up! This is *not* a drill. The University of Toronto Department of Sociology is under new management. If you'll set your handhelds to 'receive,' we'll be beaming out new lesson plans momentarily. If you've forgotten your handhelds, you can download the plans later on. I'm going to run it down for you right now, anyway.

"Before I start though, I have a prepared statement for you. You'll probably hear this a couple times more today, in your other classes. It's worth repeating. Here goes:

"We reject the stodgy, tyrannical rule of the profs at this Department. We demand bully pulpits from which to preach the Bitchun gospel. Effective immediately, the University of Toronto Ad-Hoc Sociology Department is *in charge*. We promise a high-relevance curriculum with an emphasis on reputation economies, post-scarcity social dynamics, and the social theory of infinite life-extension. No more Durkheim, kids, just deadheading! This will be *fun*."

She taught the course like a pro—you could tell she'd been drilling her lecture for a while. Periodically, the human wall behind her shuddered as the prof made a break for it and was restrained.

At precisely 9:50 A.M. she dismissed the class, which had hung on her every word. Instead of trudging out and ambling to our next class, the whole nineteen hundred of us rose, and, as one, started buzzing to our neighbors, a roar of "Can you believe it?" that followed us out the door and to our next encounter with the Ad-Hoc Sociology Department.

It was cool, that day. I had another soc class, Constructing Social Deviance, and we got the same drill there, the same stirring propaganda, the same comical sight of a tenured prof battering himself against a human wall of ad-hocs.

Reporters pounced on us when we left the class, jabbing at us with mics and peppering us with questions. I gave them a big thumbs-up and said, "Bitchun!" in classic undergrad eloquence.

The profs struck back the next morning. I got a heads-up from the newscast as I brushed my teeth: the Dean of the Department of Sociology told a reporter that the ad-hocs' courses would not be credited, that they were a gang of thugs who were totally unqualified to teach. A counterpoint interview from a spokesperson for the ad-hocs established that all of the new lecturers had been writing course-plans and lecture notes for the profs they replaced for years, and that they'd also written most of their journal articles.

The profs brought University security out to help them regain their lecterns, only to be repelled by ad-hoc security guards in homemade uniforms. University security got the message—anyone could be replaced—and stayed away.

The profs picketed. They held classes out front attended by grade-conscious brown-nosers who worried that the ad-hocs' classes wouldn't count towards their degrees. Fools like me alternated between the outdoor and indoor classes, not learning much of anything.

No one did. The profs spent their course-times whoring for Whuffie, leading the seminars like encounter groups instead of lectures. The ad-hocs spent their time badmouthing the profs and tearing apart their coursework.

At the end of the semester, everyone got a credit and the University Senate disbanded the Sociology program in favor of a distance-ed offering from Concordia in Montreal. Forty years later, the fight was settled forever. Once you took backup-and-restore, the rest of the Bitchunry just followed, a value-system settling over you.

Those who didn't take backup-and-restore may have objected, but, hey, they all died.

The Liberty Square ad-hocs marched shoulder to shoulder through the utilidors and, as a mass, took back the Haunted Mansion. Dan, Lil and I were up front, careful not to brush against one another as we walked quickly through the backstage door and started a bucket-brigade, passing out the materials that Debra's people had stashed there, along a line that snaked back to the front porch of the Hall of Presidents, where they were unceremoniously dumped.

Once the main stash was vacated, we split up and roamed the ride, its service corridors and dioramas, the break room and the secret passages, rounding up every scrap of Debra's crap and passing it out the door.

In the attic scene, I ran into Kim and three of her giggly little friends, their eyes glinting in the dim light. The gaggle of transhuman kids made my guts clench, made me think of Zed and of Lil and of my unmediated brain, and I had a sudden urge to shred them verbally.

No.

No. That way lay madness and war. This was about taking back what was ours, not punishing the interlopers. "Kim, I think you should leave," I said, quietly.

She snorted and gave me a dire look. "Who died and made you boss?" she said. Her friends thought it very brave, they made it clear with double-jointed hip-thrusts and glares.

"Kim, you can leave now or you can leave later. The longer you wait, the worse it will be for you and your Whuffie. You blew it, and you're not a part of the Mansion anymore. Go home, go to Debra. Don't stay here, and don't come back. Ever."

Ever. Be cast out of this thing that you love, that you obsess over, that you worked for. "Now," I said, quiet, dangerous, barely in control.

They sauntered into the graveyard, hissing vitriol at me. Oh, they had lots of new material to post to the anti-me sites, messages that would get them Whuffie with people who thought I was the scum of the earth. A popular view, those days.

I got out of the Mansion and looked at the bucket-brigade, followed it to the front of the Hall. The Park had been open for an hour, and a herd of guests watched the proceedings in confusion. The Liberty Square ad-hocs passed their loads around in clear embarrassment, knowing that they were violating every principle they cared about.

As I watched, gaps appeared in the bucket-brigade as castmembers slipped away, faces burning scarlet with shame. At the Hall of Presidents, Debra presided over an orderly relocation of her things, a cheerful cadre of her castmembers quickly moving it all off-stage. I didn't have to look at my handheld to know what was happening to our Whuffie.

By evening, we were back on schedule. Suneep supervised the placement of his telepresence rigs and Lil went over every system in minute detail, bossing a crew of ad-hocs that trailed behind her, double- and triple-checking it all.

Suneep smiled at me when he caught sight of me, hand-scattering dust in the parlor.

"Congratulations, sir," he said, and shook my hand. "It was masterfully done."

"Thanks, Suneep. I'm not sure how masterful it was, but we got the job done, and that's what counts."

"Your partners, they're happier than I've seen them since this whole business started. I know how they feel!"

My partners? Oh, yes, Dan and Lil. How happy were they, I wondered. Happy enough to get back together? My mood fell, even though a part of me said that Dan would never go back to her, not after all we'd been through together.

"I'm glad you're glad. We couldn't have done it without you, and it looks like we'll be open for business in a week."

"Oh, I should think so. Are you coming to the party tonight?"

Party? Probably something the Liberty Square adhocs were putting on. I would almost certainly be persona non grata. "I don't think so," I said, carefully. "I'll probably work late here."

He chided me for working too hard, but once he saw that I had no intention of being dragged to the party, he left off.

And that's how I came to be in the Mansion at 2 A.M. the next morning, dozing in a backstage break room when I heard a commotion from the parlor. Festive voices, happy and loud, and I assumed it was Liberty Square ad-hocs coming back from their party.

I roused myself and entered the parlor.

Kim and her friends were there, pushing hand trucks of Debra's gear. I got ready to shout something horrible at them, and that's when Debra came in. I moderated the shout to a snap, opened my mouth to speak, stopped.

Behind Debra were Lil's parents, frozen these long years in their canopic jars in Kissimmee.

It's a small world after all.

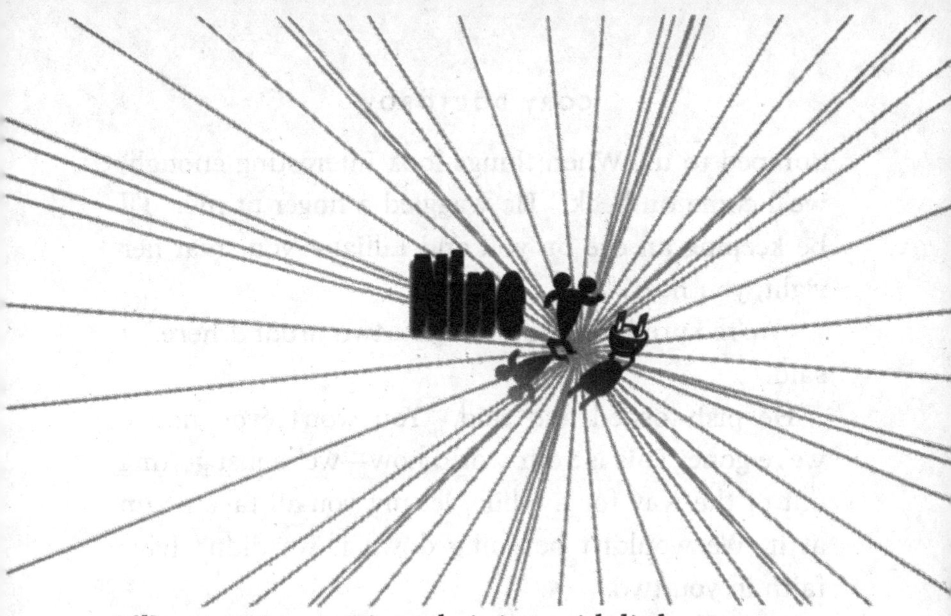

Lil's parents went into their jars with little ceremony. I saw them just before they went in, when they stopped in at Lil's and my place to kiss her good-bye and wish her well.

Tom and I stood awkwardly to the side while Lil and her mother held an achingly chipper and polite farewell.

"So," I said to Tom. "Deadheading."

He cocked an eyebrow. "Yup. Took the backup this morning."

Before coming to see their daughter, they'd taken their backups. When they woke, this event—everything following the backup—would never have happened for them.

God, they were bastards.

"When are you coming back?" I asked, keeping my castmember face on, carefully hiding away the disgust.

"We'll be sampling monthly, just getting a digest

dumped to us. When things look interesting enough, we'll come on back." He waggled a finger at me. "I'll be keeping an eye on you and Lillian—you treat her right, you hear?"

"We're sure going to miss you two around here," I said.

He pish-toshed and said, "You won't even notice we're gone. This is your world now—we're just getting out of the way for a while, letting you-all take a run at it. We wouldn't be going down if we didn't have faith in you two."

Lil and her mom kissed one last time. Her mother was more affectionate than I'd ever seen her, even to the point of tearing up a little. Here in this moment of vanishing consciousness, she could be whomever she wanted, knowing that it wouldn't matter the next time she awoke.

"Julius," she said, taking my hands, squeezing them. "You've got some wonderful times ahead of you—between Lil and the Park, you're going to have a tremendous experience, I just know it." She was infinitely serene and compassionate, and I knew it didn't count.

Still smiling, they got into their runabout and drove away to get the lethal injections, to become disembodied consciousnesses, to lose their last moments with their darling daughter.

They were not happy to be returned from the dead. Their new bodies were impossibly young, pubescent and hormonal and doleful and kitted out in the latest trendy styles. In the company of Kim and her pals, they made a solid mass of irate adolescence.

"Just what the hell do you think you're doing?" Rita asked, shoving me hard in the chest. I stumbled back into my carefully scattered dust, raising a cloud.

Rita came after me, but Tom held her back. "Julius, go away. Your actions are totally indefensible. Keep your mouth shut and go away."

I held up a hand, tried to wave away his words, opened my mouth to speak.

"Don't say a word," he said. "Leave. Now."

"Don't stay here and don't come back. Ever," Kim said, an evil look on her face.

"No," I said. "No goddamn it no. You're going to hear me out, and then I'm going to get Lil and her people and they're going to back me up. That's not negotiable."

We stared at each other across the dim parlor. Debra made a twiddling motion and the lights came up full and harsh. The expertly crafted gloom went away and it was just a dusty room with a fake fireplace.

"Let him speak," Debra said. Rita folded her arms and glared.

"I did some really awful things," I said, keeping my head up, keeping my eyes on them. "I can't excuse them, and I don't ask you to forgive them. But that doesn't change the fact that we've put our hearts and souls into this place, and it's not right to take it from us. Can't we have one constant corner of the world, one bit frozen in time for the people who love it that way? Why does your success mean our failure?

"Can't you see that we're carrying on your work? That we're tending a legacy you left us?"

"Are you through?" Rita asked.

I nodded.

"This place is not a historical preserve, Julius, it's a ride. If you don't understand that, you're in the wrong place. It's not my goddamn fault that you decided that your stupidity was on my behalf, and it doesn't make it any less stupid. All you've done is confirm my worst fears."

Debra's mask of impartiality slipped. "You stupid, deluded asshole," she said, softly. "You totter around, pissing and moaning about your little murder, your little health problems—yes, I've heard—your little fixation on keeping things the way they are. You need some perspective, Julius. You need to get away from here: Disney World isn't good for you and you're sure as hell not any good for Disney World."

It would have hurt less if I hadn't come to the same conclusion myself, somewhere along the way.

I found the ad-hoc at a Fort Wilderness campsite, sitting around a fire and singing, necking, laughing. The victory party. I trudged into the circle and hunted for Lil.

She was sitting on a log, staring into the fire, a million miles away. Lord, she was beautiful when she fretted. I stood in front of her for a minute and she stared right through me until I tapped her shoulder. She gave an involuntary squeak and then smiled at herself.

"Lil," I said, then stopped. *Your parents are home, and they've joined the other side.*

For the first time in an age, she looked at me softly, smiled even. She patted the log next to her. I sat down, felt the heat of the fire on my face, her body heat on my side. God, how did I screw this up?

Without warning, she put her arms around me and hugged me hard. I hugged her back, nose in her hair, woodsmoke smell and shampoo and sweat. "We did it," she whispered fiercely. I held onto her. *No, we didn't.*

"Lil," I said again, and pulled away.

"What?" she said, her eyes shining. She was stoned, I saw that now.

"Your parents are back. They came to the Mansion."

She was confused, shrinking, and I pressed on.

"They were with Debra."

She reeled back as if I'd slapped her.

"I told them I'd bring the whole group back to talk it over."

She hung her head and her shoulders shook, and I tentatively put an arm around her. She shook it off and sat up. She was crying and laughing at the same time. "I'll have a ferry sent over," she said.

• • •

I sat in the back of the ferry with Dan, away from the confused and angry ad-hocs. I answered his questions with terse, one-word answers, and he gave up. We rode in silence, the trees on the edges of the Seven Seas Lagoon whipping back and forth in an approaching storm.

The ad-hoc shortcutted through the west parking lot and moved through the quiet streets of Frontierland apprehensively, a funeral procession that stopped the nighttime custodial staff in their tracks.

As we drew up on Liberty Square, I saw that the work-lights were blazing and a tremendous work-gang of Debra's ad-hocs were moving from the Hall to the Mansion, undoing our teardown of their work.

Working alongside of them were Tom and Rita, Lil's parents, sleeves rolled up, forearms bulging with new, toned muscle. The group stopped in its tracks and Lil went to them, stumbling on the wooden sidewalk.

I expected hugs. There were none. In their stead, parents and daughter stalked each other, shifting weight and posture to track each other, maintain a constant, sizing distance.

"What the hell are you doing?" Lil said, finally. She didn't address her mother, which surprised me. It didn't surprise Tom, though.

He dipped forward, the shuffle of his feet loud in the quiet night. "We're working," he said.

"No, you're not," Lil said. "You're destroying. Stop it."

Lil's mother darted to her husband's side, not saying anything, just standing there.

Wordlessly, Tom hefted the box he was holding and headed to the Mansion. Lil caught his arm and jerked it so he dropped his load.

"You're not listening. The Mansion is *ours. Stop. It.*"

Lil's mother gently took Lil's hand off Tom's arm, held it in her own. "I'm glad you're passionate about it, Lillian," she said. "I'm proud of your commitment."

Even at a distance of ten yards, I heard Lil's choked sob, saw her collapse in on herself. Her mother took her in her arms, rocked her. I felt like a voyeur, but couldn't bring myself to turn away.

"Shhh," her mother said, a sibilant sound that matched the rustling of the leaves on the Liberty Tree. "Shhh. We don't have to be on the same side, you know."

They held the embrace and held it still. Lil straightened, then bent again and picked up her father's box, carried it to the Mansion. One at a time, the rest of her ad-hoc moved forward and joined them.

This is how you hit bottom. You wake up in your friend's hotel room and you power up your handheld and it won't log on. You press the call-button for the elevator and it gives you an angry buzz in return. You take the stairs to the lobby and no one looks at you as they jostle past you.

You become a non-person.

Scared. I trembled when I ascended the stairs to Dan's room, when I knocked at his door, louder and harder than I meant, a panicked banging.

Dan answered the door and I saw his eyes go to his HUD, back to me. "Jesus," he said.

I sat on the edge of my bed, head in my hands.

"What?" I said. What happened, what happened to me?

"You're out of the ad-hoc," he said. "You're out of Whuffie. You're bottomed-out," he said.

This is how you hit bottom in Walt Disney World, in a hotel with the hissing of the monorail and the sun streaming through the window, the hooting of the steam engines on the railroad and the distant howl of the recorded wolves at the Haunted Mansion. The world drops away from you, recedes until you're nothing but a speck, a mote in blackness.

I was hyperventilating, light-headed. Deliberately, I slowed my breath, put my head between my knees until the dizziness passed.

"Take me to Lil," I said.

Driving together, hammering cigarette after cigarette into my face, I remembered the night Dan had come to Disney World, when I'd driven him to my—*Lil's*—house, and how happy I'd been then, how secure.

I looked at Dan and he patted my hand. "Strange times," he said.

It was enough. We found Lil in an underground

break room, lightly dozing on a ratty sofa. Her head rested on Tom's lap, her feet on Rita's. All three snored softly. They'd had a long night.

Dan shook Lil awake. She stretched out and opened her eyes, looked sleepily at me. The blood drained from her face.

"Hello, Julius," she said, coldly.

Now Tom and Rita were awake, too. Lil sat up.

"Were you going to tell me?" I asked, quietly. "Or were you just going to kick me out and let me find out on my own?"

"You were my next stop," Lil said.

"Then I've saved you some time." I pulled up a chair. "Tell me all about it."

"There's nothing to tell," Rita snapped. "You're out. You had to know it was coming—for God's sake, you were tearing Liberty Square apart!"

"How would you know?" I asked. I struggled to remain calm. "You've been asleep for ten years!"

"We got updates," Rita said. "That's why we're back—we couldn't let it go on the way it was. We owed it to Debra."

"And Lillian," Tom said.

"And Lillian," Rita said, absently.

Dan pulled up a chair of his own. "You're not being fair to him," he said. At least someone was on my side.

"We've been more than fair," Lil said. "You know that better than anyone, Dan. We've forgiven and forgiven and forgiven, made every allowance. He's sick and he won't take the cure. There's nothing more we can do for him."

"You could be his friend," Dan said. The lightheadedness was back, and I slumped in my chair, tried to control my breathing, the panicked thumping of my heart.

"You could try to understand, you could try to help him. You could stick with him, the way he stuck with you. You don't have to toss him out on his ass."

Lil had the good grace to look slightly shamed. "I'll get him a room," she said. "For a month. In Kissimmee. A motel. I'll pick up his network access. Is that fair?"

"It's more than fair," Rita said. Why did she hate me so much? I'd been there for her daughter while she was away—ah. That might do it, all right. "I don't think it's warranted. If you want to take care of him, sir, you can. It's none of my family's business."

Lil's eyes blazed. "Let me handle this," she said. "All right?"

Rita stood up abruptly. "You do whatever you want," she said, and stormed out of the room.

"Why are you coming here for help?" Tom said, ever the voice of reason. "You seem capable enough."

"I'm going to be taking a lethal injection at the end of the week," Dan said. "Three days. That's personal, but you asked."

Tom shook his head. *Some friends you've got yourself.* I could see him thinking it.

"That soon?" Lil asked, a throb in her voice.

Dan nodded.

In a dreamlike buzz, I stood and wandered out into the utilidor, out through the western castmember parking, and away.

I wandered along the cobbled, disused Walk Around the World, each flagstone engraved with the name of a family that had visited the Park a century before. The names whipped past me like epitaphs.

The sun came up noon high as I rounded the bend of deserted beach between the Grand Floridian and the Polynesian. Lil and I had come here often, to watch the sunset from a hammock, arms around each other, the Park spread out before us like a lighted toy village.

Now the beach was deserted, the Wedding Pavilion silent. I felt suddenly cold though I was sweating freely. So cold.

Dreamlike, I walked into the lake, water filling my shoes, logging my pants, warm as blood, warm on my chest, on my chin, on my mouth, on my eyes.

I opened my mouth and inhaled deeply, water filling my lungs, choking and warm. At first I sputtered, but I was in control now, and I inhaled again. The water shimmered over my eyes, and then was dark.

I woke on Doctor Pete's cot in the Magic Kingdom, restraints around my wrists and ankles, a tube in my nose. I closed my eyes, for a moment believing that

I'd been restored from a backup, problems solved, memories behind me.

Sorrow knifed through me as I realized that Dan was probably dead by now, my memories of him gone forever.

Gradually, I realized that I was thinking nonsensically. The fact that I remembered Dan meant that I hadn't been refreshed from my backup, that my broken brain was still there, churning along in unmediated isolation.

I coughed again. My ribs ached and throbbed in counterpoint to my head. Dan took my hand.

"You're a pain in the ass, you know that?" he said, smiling.

"Sorry," I choked.

"You sure are," he said. "Lucky for you they found you—another minute or two and I'd be burying you right now."

No, I thought, confused. *They'd have restored me from backup.* Then it hit me: I'd gone on record refusing restore from backup after having it recommended by a medical professional. No one would have restored me after that. I would have been truly and finally dead. I started to shiver.

"Easy," Dan said. "Easy. It's all right now. Doctor says you've got a cracked rib or two from the CPR, but there's no brain damage."

"No *additional* brain damage," Doctor Pete said, swimming into view. He had on his professionally calm bedside face, and it reassured me despite myself.

He shooed Dan away and took his seat. Once Dan had left the room, he shone lights in my eyes and peeked in my ears, then sat back and considered me. "Well, Julius," he said. "What exactly is the problem? We can get you a lethal injection if that's what you want, but offing yourself in the Seven Seas Lagoon just isn't good show. In the meantime, would you like to talk about it?"

Part of me wanted to spit in his eye. I'd tried to talk about it and he'd told me to go to hell, and now he changes his mind? But I did want to talk.

"I didn't want to die," I said.

"Oh no?" he said. "I think the evidence suggests the contrary."

"I wasn't trying to die," I protested. "I was trying to—" What? I was trying to . . . *abdicate.* Take the refresh without choosing it, without shutting out the last year of my best friend's life. Rescue myself from the stinking pit I'd sunk into without flushing Dan away along with it. That's all, that's all.

"I wasn't thinking—I was just acting. It was an episode or something. Does that mean I'm nuts?"

"Oh, probably," Doctor Pete said, offhandedly. "But let's worry about one thing at a time. You can die if you want to, that's your right. I'd rather you lived, if you want my opinion, and I doubt that I'm the only one, Whuffie be damned. If you're going to live, I'd like to record you saying so, just in case. We have a backup of you on file—I'd hate to have to delete it."

"Yes," I said. "Yes, I'd like to be restored if there's no other option." It was true. I didn't want to die.

"All right then," Doctor Pete said. "It's on file and I'm a happy man. Now, are you nuts? Probably. A little. Nothing a little counseling and some R&R wouldn't fix, if you want my opinion. I could find you somewhere if you want."

"Not yet," I said. "I appreciate the offer, but there's something else I have to do first."

Dan took me back to the room and put me to bed with a transdermal soporific that knocked me out for the rest of the day. When I woke, the moon was over the Seven Seas Lagoon and the monorail was silent.

I stood on the patio for a while, thinking about all the things this place had meant to me for more than a century: happiness, security, efficiency, fantasy. All of it gone. It was time I left. Maybe back to space, find Zed and see if I could make her happy again. Anywhere but here. Once Dan was dead—God, it was sinking in finally—I could catch a ride down to the Cape for a launch.

"What's on your mind?" Dan asked from behind me, startling me. He was in his boxers, thin and rangy and hairy.

"Thinking about moving on," I said.

He chuckled. "I've been thinking about doing the same," he said.

I smiled. "Not that way," I said. "Just going somewhere else, starting over. Getting away from this."

"Going to take the refresh?" he asked.

I looked away. "No," I said. "I don't believe I will."

"It may be none of my business," he said, "but why the fuck not? Jesus, Julius, what're you afraid of?"

"You don't want to know," I said.

"I'll be the judge of that."

"Let's have a drink, first," I said.

Dan rolled his eyes back for a second, then said, "All right, two Coronas, coming up."

After the room service bot had left, we cracked the beers and pulled chairs out onto the porch.

"You sure you want to know this?" I asked.

He tipped his bottle at me. "Sure as shootin'," he said.

"I don't want refresh because it would mean losing the last year," I said.

He nodded. "By which you mean 'my last year,' " he said. "Right?"

I nodded and drank.

"I thought it might be like that. Julius, you are many things, but hard to figure out you are not. I have something to say that might help you make the decision. If you want to hear it, that is."

What could he have to say? "Sure," I said. "Sure." In my mind, I was on a shuttle headed for orbit, away from all of this.

"I had you killed," he said. "Debra asked me to, and I set it up. You were right all along."

The shuttle exploded in silent, slow moving space,

and I spun away from it. I opened and shut my mouth.

It was Dan's turn to look away. "Debra proposed it. We were talking about the people I'd met when I was doing my missionary work, the stone crazies who I'd have to chase away after they'd rejoined the Bitchun Society. One of them, a girl from Cheyenne Mountain, she followed me down here, kept leaving me messages. I told Debra, and that's when she got the idea.

"I'd get the girl to shoot you and disappear. Debra would give me Whuffie—piles of it, and her team would follow suit. I'd be months closer to my goal. That was all I could think about back then, you remember."

"I remember." The smell of rejuve and desperation in our little cottage, and Dan plotting my death.

"We planned it, then Debra had herself refreshed from a backup—no memory of the event, just the Whuffie for me."

"Yes," I said. That would work. Plan a murder, kill yourself, have yourself refreshed from a backup made before the plan. How many times had Debra done terrible things and erased their memories that way?

"Yes," he agreed. "We did it, I'm ashamed to say. I can prove it, too—I have my backup, and I can get Jeanine to tell it, too." He drained his beer. "That's my plan. Tomorrow. I'll tell Lil and her folks, Kim and her people, the whole ad-hoc. A going-away present from a shitty friend."

My throat was dry and tight. I drank more beer.

"You knew all along," I said. "You could have proved it at any time."

He nodded. "That's right."

"You let me . . ." I groped for the words. "You let me turn into . . ." They wouldn't come.

"I did," he said.

All this time. Lil and he, standing on *my* porch, telling me I needed help. Doctor Pete, telling me I needed refresh from backup, me saying no, no, no, not wanting to lose my last year with Dan.

"I've done some pretty shitty things in my day," he said. "This is the absolute worst. You helped me and I betrayed you. I'm sure glad I don't believe in God—that'd make what I'm going to do even scarier."

Dan was going to kill himself in two days' time. My friend and my murderer. "Dan," I croaked. I couldn't make any sense of my mind. Dan, taking care of me, helping me, sticking up for me, carrying this horrible shame with him all along. Ready to die, wanting to go with a clean conscience. "You're forgiven," I said. And it was true.

He stood.

"Where are you going" I asked.

"To find Jeanine, the one who pulled the trigger. I'll meet you at the Hall of Presidents at nine A.M."

I went in through the Main Gate, not a castmember any longer, a guest with barely enough Whuffie to scrape in, use the water fountains and stand in line. If I were lucky, a castmember might spare me a chocolate banana. Probably not, though.

I stood in the line for the Hall of Presidents. Other guests checked my Whuffie, then averted their eyes. Even the children. A year before, they'd have been striking up conversations, asking me about my job here at the Magic Kingdom.

I sat in my seat at the Hall of Presidents, watching the short film with the rest, sitting patiently while they rocked in their seats under the blast of the flash-bake. A castmember picked up the stage side mic and thanked everyone for coming; the doors swung open and the Hall was empty, except for me. The castmember narrowed her eyes at me, then recognizing me, turned her back and went to show in the next group.

No group came. Instead, Dan and the girl I'd seen on the replay entered.

"We've closed it down for the morning," he said.

I was staring at the girl, seeing her smirk as she pulled the trigger on me, seeing her now with a contrite, scared expression. She was terrified of me.

"You must be Jeanine," I said. I stood and shook her hand. "I'm Julius."

Her hand was cold, and she took it back and wiped it on her pants.

My castmember instincts took over. "Please, have a seat. Don't worry, it'll all be fine. Really. No hard feelings." I stopped short of offering to get her a glass of water.

Put her at her ease, said a snotty voice in my head. *She'll make a better witness. Or make her nervous, pathetic—that'll work, too; make Debra look even worse.*

I told the voice to shut up and got her a cup of water.

By the time I came back, the whole gang was there, Debra, Lil, her folks, Tim. Debra's gang and Lil's gang, now one united team. Soon to be scattered.

Dan took the stage, used the stageside mic to broadcast his voice. "Eleven months ago, I did an awful thing. I plotted with Debra to have Julius murdered. I used a friend who was a little confused at the time, used her to pull the trigger. It was Debra's idea that having Julius killed would cause enough confusion that she could take over the Hall of Presidents. It did."

There was a roar of conversation. I looked at Debra, saw that she was sitting calmly, as though Dan had just accused her of sneaking an extra helping of dessert. Lil's parents, to either side of her, were less sanguine. Tom's jaw was set and angry, Rita was speaking angrily to Debra. Hickory Jackson in the old Hall used to say, *I will hang the first man I can lay hands on from the first tree I can find.*

"Debra had herself refreshed from backup after we planned it," Dan went on, as though no one was talking. "I was supposed to do the same, but I didn't. I have a backup in my public directory—anyone can examine it. Right now, I'd like to bring Jeanine up, she's got a few words she'd like to say."

I helped Jeanine take the stage. She was still trembling, and the ad-hocs were an insensate babble of recriminations. Despite myself, I was enjoying it.

"Hello," Jeanine said softly. She had a lovely voice, a lovely face. I wondered if we could be friends when it was all over. She probably didn't care much about Whuffie, one way or another.

The discussion went on. Dan took the mic from her and said, "Please! Can we have a little respect for our visitor? Please? People?"

Gradually, the din decreased. Dan passed the mic back to Jeanine. "Hello," she said again, and flinched from the sound of her voice in the Hall's PA. "My name is Jeanine. I'm the one who killed Julius, a year ago. Dan asked me to, and I did it. I didn't ask why. I trusted—trust—him. He told me that Julius would make a backup a few minutes before I shot him, and that he could get me out of the Park without getting caught. I'm very sorry." There was something off-kilter about her, some stilt to her stance and words that let you know she wasn't all there. Growing up in a mountain might do that to you. I snuck a look at Lil, whose lips were pressed together. Growing up in a themepark might do that to you, too.

"Thank you, Jeanine," Dan said, taking back the mic. "You can have a seat now. I've said everything I need to say—Julius and I have had our own discussions in private. If there's anyone else who'd like to speak—"

The words were barely out of his mouth before the crowd erupted again in words and waving hands. Beside me, Jeanine flinched. I took her hand and shouted in her ear: "Have you ever been on the Pirates of the Carribean?"

She shook her head.

I stood up and pulled her to her feet. "You'll love it," I said, and led her out of the Hall.

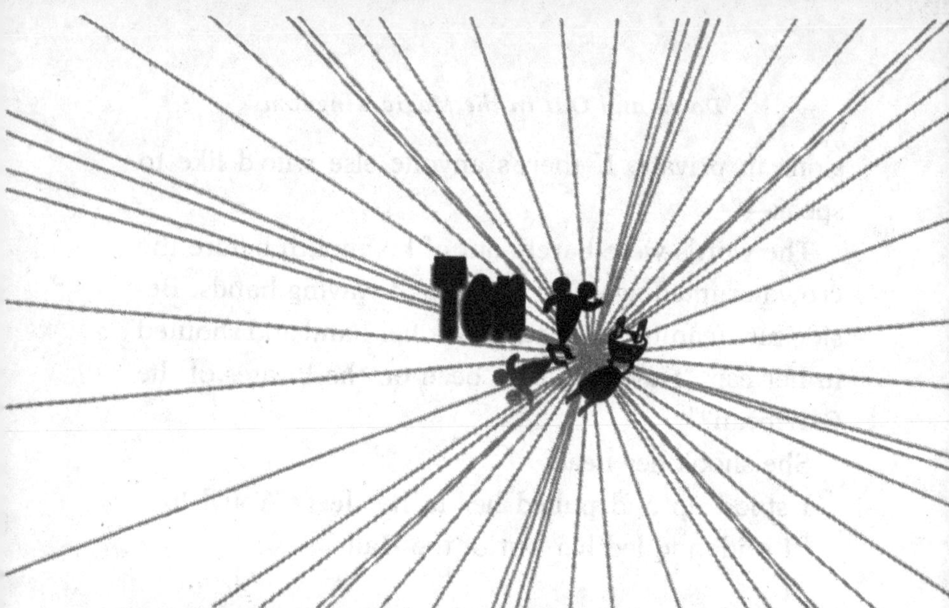

I booked us ringside seats at the Polynesian Luau, riding high on a fresh round of sympathy Whuffie, and Dan and I drank a dozen lapu-lapus in hollowed-out pineapples before giving up on the idea of getting drunk.

Jeanine watched the fire-dances and the torch-lighting with eyes like saucers, and picked daintily at her spare ribs with one hand, never averting her attention from the floor show. When they danced the fast hula, her eyes jiggled. I chuckled.

From where we sat, I could see the spot where I'd waded into the Seven Seas Lagoon and breathed in the blood-temp water, I could see Cinderella's Castle, across the lagoon, I could see the monorails and the ferries and the busses making their busy way through the Park, shuttling teeming masses of guests from place to place. Dan toasted me with his pineapple and I toasted him back, drank it dry and belched in satisfaction.

Full belly, good friends, and the sunset behind a troupe of tawny, half-naked hula dancers. Who needs the Bitchun Society, anyway?

When it was over, we watched the fireworks from the beach, my toes dug into the clean white sand. Dan slipped his hand into my left hand, and Jeanine took my right. When the sky darkened and the lighted barges puttered away through the night, we three sat in the hammock.

I looked out over the Seven Seas Lagoon and realized that this was my last night, ever, in Walt Disney World. It was time to reboot again, start afresh. That's what the Park was for, only somehow, this visit, I'd gotten stuck. Dan had unstuck me.

The talk turned to Dan's impending death.

"So, tell me what you think of this," he said, hauling away on a glowing cigarette.

"Shoot," I said.

"I'm thinking—why take lethal injection? I mean, I may be done here for now, but why should I make an irreversible decision?"

"Why did you want to before?" I asked.

"Oh, it was the macho thing, I guess. The finality and all. But hell, I don't have to prove anything, right?"

"Sure," I said, magnanimously.

"So," he said, thoughtfully. "The question I'm asking is, how long can I deadhead for? There are folks who go down for a thousand years, ten thousand, right?"

"So, you're thinking, what, a million?" I joked.

He laughed. "A *million?* You're thinking too small, son. Try this on for size: the heat death of the universe."

"The heat death of the universe," I repeated.

"Sure," he drawled, and I sensed his grin in the dark. "Ten to the hundred years or so. The Stelliferous Period—it's when all the black holes have run dry and things get, you know, stupendously dull. Cold, too. So I'm thinking—why not leave a wake-up call for some time around then?"

"Sounds unpleasant to me," I said. "Brrrr."

"Not at all! I figure, self-repairing nano-based canopic jar, mass enough to feed it—say, a trillion-ton asteroid—and a lot of solitude when the time comes around. I'll poke my head in every century or so, just to see what's what, but if nothing really stupendous crops up, I'll take the long ride out. The final frontier."

"That's pretty cool," Jeanine said.

"Thanks," Dan said.

"You're not kidding, are you?" I asked.

"Nope, I sure ain't," he said.

They didn't invite me back into the ad-hoc, even after Debra left in Whuffie-penury and they started to put the Mansion back the way it was. Tim called me to say that with enough support from Imagineering, they thought they could get it up and running in a week. Suneep was ready to kill someone, I swear. *A house* *divided against itself can* not *stand,* as Mr. Lincoln used to say at the Hall of Presidents.

I packed three changes of clothes and a toothbrush in my shoulderbag and checked out of my suite at the Polynesian at ten A.M., then met Jeanine and Dan at the valet parking out front. Dan had a runabout he'd picked up with my Whuffie, and I piled in with Jeanine in the middle. We played old Beatles tunes on the stereo all the long way to Cape Canaveral. Our shuttle lifted at noon.

The shuttle docked four hours later, but by the time we'd been through decontam and orientation, it was suppertime. Dan, nearly as Whuffie-poor as Debra after his confession, nevertheless treated us to a meal in the big bubble, squeeze-tubes of heady booze and steaky paste, and we watched the universe get colder for a while.

There were a couple guys jamming, tethered to a guitar and a set of tubs, and they weren't half bad.

Jeanine was uncomfortable hanging there naked. She'd gone to space with her folks after Dan had left the mountain, but it was in a long-haul generation ship. She'd abandoned it after a year or two and deadheaded back to Earth in a support-pod. She'd get used to life in space after a while. Or she wouldn't.

"Well," Dan said.

"Yup," I said, aping his laconic drawl. He smiled.

"It's that time," he said.

Spheres of saline tears formed in Jeanine's eyes, and

I brushed them away, setting them adrift in the bubble. I'd developed some real tender, brother-sister type feelings for her since I'd watched her saucer-eye her way through the Magic Kingdom. No romance—not for me, thanks! But camaraderie and a sense of responsibility.

"See you in ten to the hundred," Dan said, and headed to the airlock. I started after him, but Jeanine caught my hand.

"He hates long good-byes," she said.

"I know," I said, and watched him go.

The universe gets older. So do I. So does my backup, sitting in redundant distributed storage dirtside, ready for the day that space or age or stupidity kills me. It recedes with the years, and I write out my life longhand, a letter to the me that I'll be when it's restored into a clone somewhere, somewhen. It's important that whoever I am then knows about this year, and it's going to take a lot of tries for me to get it right.

In the meantime, I'm working on another symphony, one with a little bit of "Grim Grinning Ghosts," and a nod to "It's a Small World After All," and especially "There's a Great Big Beautiful Tomorrow."

Jeanine says it's pretty good, but what does she know? She's barely fifty.

We've both got a lot of living to do before we know what's what.

Acknowledgments

I could never have written this book without the personal support of my friends and family, especially Roz Doctorow, Gord Doctorow and Neil Doctorow, Amanda Foubister, Steve Samenski, Pat York, Grad Conn, John Henson, John Rose, the writers at the Cecil Street Irregulars, and Mark Frauenfelder.

I owe a great debt to the writers and editors who mentored and encouraged me: James Patrick Kelly, Judith Merril, Damon Knight, Martha Soukup, Scott Edelman, Gardner Dozois, Renee Wilmeth, Teresa Nielsen Hayden, Claire Eddy, Bob Parks, and Robert Killheffer.

I am also indebted to my editor, Patrick Nielsen Hayden, and my agent, Donald Maass, who believed in this book and helped me bring it to fruition.

Finally, I must thank the readers, the geeks, and the Imagineers who inspired this book.

CORY DOCTOROW
San Francisco
September 2002